MILADY TOOK
THE RAP

THE CLASSIC HANK JANSON

The first original Hank Janson book appeared in 1946, and the last in 1971. However, the classic era on which we are focusing in the Telos reissue series lasted from 1946 to 1953. The following is a checklist of those books, which were subdivided into five main series and a number of 'specials'.

PRE-SERIES BOOKS
When Dames Get Tough (1946)
Scarred Faces (1947)

SERIES ONE
1) This Woman Is Death (1948)
2) Lady, Mind That Corpse (1948)
3) Gun Moll For Hire (1948)
4) No Regrets For Clara (194)
5) Smart Girls Don't Talk (1949)
6) Lilies For My Lovely (1949)
7) Blonde On The Spot (1949)
8) Honey, Take My Gun (1949)
9) Sweetheart, Here's Your Grave (1949)
10) Gunsmoke In Her Eyes (1949)
11) Angel, Shoot To Kill (1949)
12) Slay-Ride For Cutie (1949)

SERIES TWO
13) Sister, Don't Hate Me (1949)
14) Some Look Better Dead (1950)
15) Sweetie, Hold Me Tight (1950)
16) Torment For Trixie (1950)
17) Don't Dare Me, Sugar (1950)
18) The Lady Has A Scar (1950)
19) The Jane With The Green Eyes (1950)
20) Lola Brought Her Wreath (1950)
21) Lady, Toll The Bell (1950)
22) The Bride Wore Weeds (1950)
23) Don't Mourn Me Toots (1951)
24) This Dame Dies Soon (1951)

SERIES THREE
25) Baby, Don't Dare Squeal (1951)
26) Death Wore A Petticoat (1951)
27) Hotsy, You'll Be Chilled (1951)

28) It's Always Eve That Weeps (1951)
29) Frails Can Be So Tough (1951)
30) Milady Took The Rap (1951)
31) Women Hate Till Death (1951)
32) Broads Don't Scare Easy (1951)
33) Skirts Bring Me Sorrow (1951)
34) Sadie Don't Cry Now (1952)
35) The Filly Wore A Rod (1952)
36) Kill Her If You Can (1952)

SERIES FOUR
37) Murder (1952)
38) Conflict (1952)
39) Tension (1952)
40) Whiplash (1952)
41) Accused (1952)
42) Killer (1952)
43) Suspense (1952)
44) Pursuit (1953)
45) Vengeance (1953)
46) Torment (1953)
47) Amok (1953)
48) Corruption (1953)

SERIES FIVE
49) Silken Menace (1953)
50) Nyloned Avenger (1953)

SPECIALS
Auctioned (1952)
Persian Pride (1952)
Desert Fury (1953)
One Man In His Time (1953)
Unseen Assassin (1953)
Deadly Mission (1953)

MILADY TOOK
THE RAP

HANK JANSON

This edition published in 2021 by
Telos Moonrise: Criminal Pursuits
(An imprint of Telos Publishing)
139 Whitstable Road, Canterbury, Kent CT2 8EQ,
United Kingdom.

www.telos.co.uk

ISBN: 978-1-84583-192-9

Telos Publishing Ltd values feedback. Please e-mail any
comments you might have about this book to:
feedback@telos.co.uk

Novel by Stephen D Frances
Cover by Reginald Heade
Silhouette device by Philip Mendoza

The Hank Janson name, logo and silhouette device are
registered trademarks of Telos Publishing Ltd.

First published in England by
New Fiction Press, September 1951

British Library Cataloguing in Publication Data.
A catalogue record for this book is available from the British
Library.

HANK JANSON

PUBLISHER'S NOTE

The appeal of the Hank Janson books to a modern readership lies not only in the quality of the storytelling, which is as powerfully compelling today as it was when they were first published, but also in the fascinating insight they afford into the attitudes, customs and morals of the 1940s and 1950s. We have therefore endeavoured to make *Milady Takes the Rap*, and all our other Hank Janson reissues, as faithful to the original editions as possible. Unlike some other publishers, who when reissuing vintage fiction have been known to edit it to remove aspects that might offend present-day sensibilities, we have left the original narrative absolutely intact.

The original editions of these classic Hank Janson titles made quite frequent use of phonetic 'Americanisms' such as 'kinda', 'gotta', 'wanna' and so on. Again, we have left these unchanged in the Telos Publishing reissues, to give readers as genuine as possible a taste of what it was like to read these books when they first came out, even though such devices have since become sorta out of fashion.

The only way in which we have amended the original text has been to correct obvious lapses in spelling, grammar and punctuation, and to remedy clear typesetting errors (such as the fact that, in the original edition of *Milady Took the Rap*, there were two chapters numbered eleven!)

5

ABOUT THE COVER

Milady Took the Rap was the second Hank Janson title to be published by New Fiction Press, an imprint of Editions Poetry (London) Ltd, after its owner Reginald Carter acquired the rights to the series from its creator and true author Stephen Frances. It was also the second of a run of five to appear without one of the sensational Reginald Heade cover paintings that were a big part of the series' appeal; instead, it had just the cover text and the Philip Mendoza-designed Hank Janson silhouette logo placed against a plain red background (right). This was a move

made by Carter to try to avoid incurring the wrath of the British authorities, who at the time were clamping down on such 'racy' pulp paperbacks, resulting in copies of many examples being seized and destroyed by the police, and some of those responsible for their publication being prosecuted under the Obscene Publications Act. Prior to this act of self-censorship, Heade had actually completed a cover painting for the book, and copies of that originally-intended version had even been printed up, with the 1/6 price that Heade had added (a standard part of his assignment) silvered over with the new regular 2/- price that Carter had just decided to adopt. To avoid wasting paper – a particularly valuable commodity in the post-war years – those now-unwanted copies of the abandoned first version of the cover were subsequently overprinted for use on contemporary 'silhouette reissues' of other Hank Janson titles, including *The Jane With Green Eyes* – although in some cases the original artwork was still faintly visible beneath the new, giving readers a tantalising glimpse of what might have been (right top). Heade's artwork did eventually see print some two years later, repurposed for use on a '12th Edition' reissue of a different Hank Janson novel, *Lilies for My Lovely*, with the new title and price rather clumsily superimposed over the old (right below).

This Telos Publishing reissue of *Milady Took the Rap* is the first to have a recreation of the originally-intended cover restored to its rightful place. As the adapted *Lilies for My Lovely* version of Heade's artwork is the only one of which an image is known to have survived, the colour he used for the *Milady Took the Rap* title lettering is uncertain (although the 1/6 price was definitely in green); yellow has been chosen for this restoration, as that was a typical preference of his at the time, but it is possible that it was originally a darker colour.

As it turned out, Reginald Carter's attempt to avoid problems with the authorities proved fruitless, as *Milady Took the Rap* incurred 15 police destruction orders and was the first of the Hank Janson titles to land him in court on a charge of obscenity. A guilty plea was entered, and the publisher was fined £100 plus costs. A short while later, *Milady Took the Rap* and *The Jane With Green Eyes* were both the subject of another, similar prosecution, this time against Stephen Frances, who had admitted to the police that he was their author. Frances appeared in court on 22 January 1953, having travelled back to England from his adopted home country of Spain in order to do so, and was found guilty on both counts. He was fined £50 plus costs for each of the two books.[1]

Ironically, for reasons unknown, neither the *Milady Took the Rap* title nor Heade's original cover artwork for the novel bears any relation to the story actually presented within.

---

[1] Anyone interested in learning more about this subject should seek out a copy of Steve Holland's *The Trials of Hank Janson* (Telos Publishing, 2005).

1

If you want to visit the brightest, noisiest, warmest, most crowded and most interesting place on Earth, I recommend the fairground on Long View Beach, Florida.

It's a long hop from Chicago to Florida. But if you've got the dough and the inclination, it's worthwhile for many reasons. I had the dough and I found it worthwhile.

It was a cold, grey day in Chicago when I climbed aboard the aircraft. It had been threatening snow for hours and the first few flakes whirled against the windows as the props began to turn. Much later, when I stepped out of the aircraft, hot sun drove at me from a clear blue sky. I got the kinda pleased feeling a guy would get who's been transported from hell to paradise.

The trip wasn't my idea. It was the Chief's idea. He figured I'd been working hard during the last few months and needed a holiday.

'It's for your own good, Hank,' he told me, rolling his cigar from one corner of his mouth to the other. 'Lie in the sun for a few weeks, soak up some Florida sunshine. A guy can work just so long. After that he isn't working, he's killing himself.'

I grinned. 'I feel healthy for a potential corpse.'

But he didn't grin back. He frowned. 'I'm on the level, Hank,' he said seriously. 'In recent months you've been in things right up to the neck. You've been turning in hot copy that nearly burnt down the joint a dozen times. But ...' he broke off, shook his head slowly and doubtfully.

I became anxious, felt the grin slip from my face. I went around his side of the desk, grasped him by the shoulder. 'Now, wait a minute, Chief,' I said grimly. 'Don't let's have doubletalk. Let me have it straight. You saying I'm going stale or something?'

This time he did grin. But his wide blue eyes remained serious. 'You're not going stale, Hank.' he said. 'The stuff you're writing is as good as ever. But we can't expect the impossible. Don't drive yourself too hard. You've gotta give yourself a chance. Your body's like a car, it'll give excellent performance for years if you treat it right. But if you don't handle it right, you can burn the guts out of a good car in a week.'

'Listen, Chief,' I said grimly. 'When my copy gets bad, start squawking. Until then, clam up.'

He sighed wearily. 'Look,' he pleaded. 'All I'm asking is you take a few weeks' vacation. Do I have to go on hands and knees?'

'Aw, shucks, Chief,' I growled. 'I'm doing okay. I'm in a groove. I'm getting along nicely. I don't need no changes.'

He sighed again. 'D'you know what I'd like right now, Hank?'

'A blonde, a bottle of champagne and a studio couch,' I guessed.

'Right now,' he said with relish, 'I'd like some nice fella to suggest I take a nice long vacation in Florida. I'm good and tired. I could use a vacation like that.'

'That's fine, Chief,' I said. 'Now just you climb outta that chair. You haven't a thing to worry about. I'll have the girl get the tickets for you. You can leave tomorrow.' I bent down, polished the arm of his chair with my sleeve. 'Boy, oh boy,' I gloated. 'Here's my chance to sit where I've always wanted.'

I was ribbing. He knew it. But he didn't grin. 'That's just the way it is, Hank,' he said seriously.

I stared at him. 'What are you talking about?'

'I want you to take over. Like I said, I've been needing a vacation. I've gotta have somebody I can rely on to take over while I'm gone. You're the guy to do it.'

I stared at him wide-eyed. 'You really mean that!'

He raised his eyes to heaven. 'Sure, sure,' he said. 'I know. A few weeks with you in the chair and it won't be the same paper. I'll come back, find the place cordoned off by the cops and you in jail. Or maybe the military holding back the angry mobs trying to burn the place down.' He shrugged his shoulders. 'It's a risk, I know. But one thing's certain. Whatever else happens, the circulation won't drop under you. I can't say that of anyone else.'

'You really on the level about me taking over while you're away?'

'On the level, Hank,' he said. He wasn't joking anymore.

'I'll take care of it,' I promised sincerely. 'I won't let you down.'

'I know that, Hank,' he said.

We weren't play-acting any longer. We were talking as friends. I'd given him my assurance I would play square by him. He'd accepted my assurance.

'You'll have to straighten me out on one or two things before you leave,' I told him.

'Plenty of time for that when you get back from Florida.'

'But ...' I began.

'Like I said, Hank,' he said wearily 'You're gonna take a trip to Florida. Sitting behind this desk may look easy to you right now. But it'll feel different when this chair's pressed up hard against the slack of your pants. I want you to start fresh. I want you to have a complete change, forget about news, forget about reporting, forget about everything connected with the newspaper game for a few weeks. I want you to come back fresh, full of vigour and as smart as paint. And I want you to do a job I'm gonna be proud of.'

'I don't need any break,' I told him. 'I can start in right now. All you've got to do is ...'

His blue eyes hardened and his forehead wrinkled as he scowled heavily. 'Now just you look here,' he said. 'I'm the guy that's running this paper. And when I tell you that you're ...'

The Chief got his way. He always does when he's set on it. That's how it was I found myself stepping out of the plane into the bright sunshine of Florida with three or four weeks of leisure stretching ahead of me and simply nothing to do. Nothing to do!

Having nothing to do was the reason I found myself on my first night in Long View, wandering around the fairground. In fact, wherever you happen to be staying in Long View, the chances are you'll spend some part of your evening wandering around the fairground. Because, apart from a dance hall, a few open air cafés and a pool saloon, the fairground monopolises the evening's attractions.

I'd rented a beach villa and the services of a coloured cook. After she'd served dinner, her day was through. She left me alone listening to the radio, and when I got bored with that, the sound of the sea lapping on the silvery sands.

It was a warm night. I went out with my white jacket over my arm and sweat sticking my shirt to my shoulders.

The fairground was a coupla miles along the beach. The shower of bright lights beckoned irresistibly. I could have walked the other way, walked into the silence and the darkness that seemed to extend never-endingly. But human beings are social animals. They like to associate with their own kind. Those bright lights had an appeal I couldn't resist.

I hadn't realised how big the fairground was. The nearer I got, the further away it seemed, the lights grew bigger and brighter and the strains of the hurdy-gurdies and the organ music became louder and louder When I finally found myself shouldering my way through the crowds with the bright lights blazing in my eyes, I was almost deafened.

But it was pleasant there. Choc-a-block with holidaymakers, it had a happy, cheerful atmosphere, exerted a warming, devil-may-care feeling. There wasn't anybody who hadn't a smile.

High above my head, the rollercoaster tore into sharp bends, swooped into the depths with a loud, thunderous roar, shrill shrieks of feminine excitement lingering on the air behind it. The roundabout hurdy-gurdy bravely blazoned Sousa's march as inevitable pole-transfixed wooden horses plunged in their circular canter. The barkers' voices rolled around my ears in urgent competition, girlish shrieks echoed from the Tunnel of Love, a coloured boy with an expansive, white-toothed grin thrust a steaming offering beneath my nose with the invitation, 'Hot dog, mister,' while the sharp crack of rifles on the target range punctuated the background.

'Not hungry, kid,' I grinned; but at the same time I was delving into my pocket. I spun a half-dollar so it flashed in the air. He caught it neatly and his grin was twice as wide. 'Thank yuh, sir,' he grinned, big eyes gleaming with gratefulness.

I sauntered to the nearest booth. Coconut shies. I stood and stared at it. All kinds of little-remembered instincts were battling inside me. I was a grown man, an adult who shortly was to have the responsibility of editing one of Chicago's biggest newspapers. Yet strange boyish impulses were thrilling inside me, old memories reviving a forgotten nostalgia. I was reliving the thrilling excitement of a 12-year-old boy paying his first visit to a circus. Before I knew it, I was handing over dough, accepting wooden balls that, now I held them, seemed absurdly small and light.

I don't know what's so strange about a guy buying himself a few shies at a coconut. It was probably my imagination, but it seemed half the fairground gathered round to watch. Young guys with their dolls, old fellas who sucked at well-worn pipes or chewed tobacco emotionlessly, and a coupla dames, arm-in-arm, who watched me solemnly, like I was a lecturer about to impart valuable information. Right next to them were three giggling girls who should have been wearing gymslips. They were wearing high-heels and lipstick instead. They couldn't have been more than 15, but acted as sex-hungry as wolves. They kept looking at me admiringly, giggling among themselves. I felt my face turn red.

I fought down embarrassment, gripped the first ball securely and put all my beef behind it. Light though it was, it hit the backcloth like a cannonball, nearly made a hole in the canvas. It was about six feet too high!

There was a united giggle from the teenagers.

I turned, stared at them. One of them, with black expressive eyes, used her eyes even more expressively. Can you beat that? A kid giving me the come-on! I glared, and she lowered her eyes demurely, half-turned to her friends, who were already giggling shrilly, clutching at each other.

My face would have taken first prize in a beetroot competition as I got ready to throw the second ball. I hated the whole damned set-up now. I wished I'd never seen a coconut shy. I aimed hurriedly, and threw angrily. There were grunts and low chuckles as the ball soared over the background cloth. The Barker scowled darkly, motioned to his boy, who went running off to find the ball.

Cold shivers travelled down my back as girlish laughter echoed behind me once more.

I didn't even try to aim the rest of the balls. I tossed them one after the other, swiftly, angrily and without aim. As the last ball left my hand, I turned away quickly, started to thrust my way through the crowds.

'Just a minute, mister,' yelled the barker. 'Just a minute, sir.' I tried to ignore him. His voice rose even louder, demanding and insistent. 'Just a minute, sir. Come back, if you please.'

Half my audience would chase after me if I didn't turn back. I tried to look at him without noticing the teenager with the expressive black eyes. I hadn't a chance. She was right behind me. As I turned, I bumped into her. As I mumbled a red-faced apology, she was putting in more hard work with her eyes. Her two friends were clutching her excitedly, eyes sparkling with daring.

'Your coconut,' said the barker. 'You knocked over a coconut.' He thrust it at me. It was big, rough-haired and the first I'd won in my life. There was a time when I'd have been transported to the realms of ecstasy by winning a coconut. Right then, the first time I'd won a coconut, I hated the damn thing.

Expressive Eyes said admiringly, 'Gee, Mister. You sure know how to roll them over!'

I looked at her. I looked at her two friends. They stared back

14

at me solemnly like they was waiting for something to happen. It seemed like a hundred other eyes were watching too.

'Sure,' I said gruffly. 'Sure, sure.' I turned away brusquely, pushed my way through the crowd. I still carried my coconut. Just ahead of me was the roundabout. There was a prickly sensation at the back of my neck, a warning I've had before when being followed. I tensed, spun around quickly.

I *was* being followed. Those three damned kids. They stared at me, giggled, whispered to each other, giggled some more. The one with expressive eyes looked at me through her eyelashes. And the devil of it! Her expression was a dead ringer for a Myrna Loy-style sexy invitation.

How d'you behave with three kids like that? I said loudly, 'Hey, you. You like coconuts? Huh?'

They looked at each other, giggled sheepishly. One said, 'Yes, please, mister. We like coconuts.'

'Catch,' I said. I tossed it; one of them caught it.

The girl with the expressive eyes drawled, 'Gee, mister. We like you, too!'

I gulped, turned quickly and threaded my way through the crowds. I still had that prickly feeling on the back of my neck. It wouldn't go away. With good reason. They followed right behind me. I plunged into the crowd at its thickest. But they were slighter than me. Where I thrust with my shoulders, they slipped through easily like quicksilver. Ten minutes later, my shirt was sticking to my shoulders, my forehead was damp and they were still right behind me. Running from them hadn't succeeded. I'd have to try strategy.

I turned around, sauntered back to them. 'Hello, kids,' I said genially.

'Hello, mister,' they chorused.

'Be good kids,' I pleaded. 'Quit following me, will ya?'

Expressive Eyes looked through her eyelashes, moved one shoulder gracefully toward me and held her hand poised like a fashion model's. 'What's your name?' she drawled archly.

I breathed hard. I preserved the genial tone in my voice though. 'How would you kids like to grab yourself a ride on some of these swings?' As I spoke, I fumbled in my pocket, pulled out a coupla dollar bills.

They stared at me solemnly, eyes flicking from the dollar bills to my face.

'How about it, kids?' I urged. 'Grab yourself a ride on something, huh?' I pushed the dollar bills toward Expressive Eyes. She looked at them, eyes gleaming. Her fingers itched to reach for them.

'Aw, Elsie,' said one, in an outraged voice. 'You can't take money. Not from a strange man. You can't do that, Elsie!'

Elsie's itching fingers fell to her sides reluctantly. 'Thanks, mister. But we couldn't do that.' Then her black eyes narrowed, her lips became provocative and inviting. 'We'd go for a ride with you if you asked us, mister.'

'I'd like to take you kids,' I said, 'but I'm busy right now. What say you go by yourselves? Have fun, huh?'

Elsie leaned toward me, face uptilted toward mine impudently. What I could see of her black eyes through those narrowed eyelashes gleamed sulky and passionate. 'I'd like to go for a ride with you, mister,' she drawled again. 'Take me, will ya? Take me on the Tunnel of Love.'

Her friends giggled explosively, held tight to one another. Elsie leaned even more closely, moistened her red lips and fluttered her eyelashes.

Can you beat that? Me a grown man and those kids of 15 tracking me down, stalking me so I was almost running from them. My cheeks flamed, and protectively I turned away, tried to lose them in the crowds.

They stuck like glue. They did better. Whenever they got level with me, Elsie tried holding my arm. 'Don't be so stuffy,' she pleaded. 'You're just the kinda fella I'd like for a date!'

I became desperate. I didn't feel one little bit like a strong-minded, self-assertive male. I felt like a jungle rabbit, methodically stalked by three snarling, dangerous tigresses.

I had to ditch those kids somehow before I was picked up for baby-snatching. Every minute they were growing more and more daring, more and more determined. And every minute I was becoming more and more desperate.

It was the dame with the red blouse who gave me the idea. She was standing with her back toward me, sadly watching gaily-coloured dodgem cars manoeuvring around each other. She also wore a black flared skirt that fitted tightly around her hips, fell in neat folds that emphasised the contours of her thighs. At first glance it looked like an A1 body the skirt was covering.

For the fifteenth time I disengaged my arm from Elsie's squeezing hand. 'Listen, you three,' I said angrily. 'My wife's waiting for me over there. She's mighty jealous. Don't say I haven't warned you.'

There was a kinda numbed silence. The three of them exchanged glances. Then Elsie said defiantly, 'I don't believe she's your wife. You're just being stuffy.'

I had to do something. Those three kids were set on romance. They'd maybe follow me all evening, maybe follow me home! My heart chilled as I remembered I was alone in the villa. With a kinda grim desperation I shook off Elsie's eager fingers, took long, rapid strides toward the dame with the red blouse. I took her by the shoulder, twisted her around. She turned easily, like she was half expecting it. I didn't see her face, but because she turned so easily the natural thing was to kiss her. That's just what I did. She kissed right back, like it was what she'd been waiting for all her life. It lasted only a coupla seconds, because while it's a dame's natural instinct to respond to being kissed, there's also a natural desire to know who's doing the kissing. She pushed herself away so she could get a good look at me. That was when I got a good look at her!

Not everybody can be beautiful. And when you've been around as much as I have, a dame has to be really repulsive to produce a shudder. The red blouse and the flared black skirt covering feminine curves had given her a big build-up. It was cruel of nature to give her the face she had. I won't say I blanched; but I sure had to keep a tight hold of myself. She had a vinegary, metallic face with every feature out of proportion. She had a wart, too. Her only redeeming features were her eyes.

They were nice eyes.

I gulped. 'I … er … I … I'm so sorry …'

I was looking at her and the three kids at the same time. The kids were standing at a distance, watching sullenly, carefully weighing up every fleeting expression on my face.

'I'm sorry,' I mumbled again. 'I thought you were somebody I knew, and …'

She had nice eyes. They mirrored her swiftly-changing impressions; surprise, indignation, then back to surprise; swift appraisal, approval and then good humour.

'Well, I never did,' she said breathlessly. She was smiling now. Her eyes sparkled as though at unexpected good fortune.

I shot a quick glance at the three kids. They were still waiting and watching doggedly.

I worked up a smile, tried to look as though I was apologising for keeping her waiting. 'I could have sworn … I mean … well … from behind, you looked just like somebody I knew, and …'

'It would have been a nice surprise for them,' she said. Her voice was quiet, well-modulated, a nice voice.

'I do hope you will forgive me.'

'It was certainly a surprise,' she chuckled. Her eyes twinkled. 'But not exactly unpleasant.'

The three kids were still watching doggedly. I said quickly, eagerly, 'Do be a sport. Try out one of these dodgem cars with me, will you?'

Her eyes widened. She'd looked in her mirror. She knew what I could see. The betting was high she hadn't many guys issuing her invitations. She accepted with alacrity. 'Well, if that's what you'd like …'

The dodgem cars were starting a new round. I took her by the elbow, steered her into a vacant car. I sat back, left her to drive. She was excited and thrilled. I felt mean, stringing her along that way. She was experiencing the excited thrill of a date, and I knew right then I was gonna disappoint her.

The three kids were waiting when we came off the dodgems. They were silent, sullen and watching. They kept looking at the dame with disbelief in their eyes. I took her by the arm, steered her quickly in the opposite direction. That brought us to the rollercoaster.

'Let's try this,' I said.

'Promise you'll hold me if I look like falling?'

'I'll take care of you,' I promised. She had a nice voice, nice eyes. If only I hadn't had to keep looking at her face! At that wart!

That rollercoaster was a terror. She shrieked when we swooped madly downwards, leaned breathlessly against me when the cogged wheels pulled us up the steep slope, on toward the next plunge earthwards. When she leaned against me there was a softness about her, a kinda intimacy that showed she was warmed by our contact.

She was laughing and gasping when the coaster rolled to a stop. She held my arm, I teased her good-naturedly. The three kids stood and watched us sullenly. I wondered if I'd ever get rid of them. I steered her toward the Tunnel of Love. The two-seater cars made their entrance to the tunnel singly. We climbed into the next vacant car, the attendant adjusted the strap that prevented us falling out, and right behind him the three kids were watching me with undisguised contempt. As the car got into movement, Elsie tossed her head scornfully, contemptuously threw my coconut to one side. The three of them turned away. Their attitude said plainer than words that they figured I was a hopeless case if I was gonna take this dame into the Tunnel of Love.

We sped into the darkness, cobwebs drifted across our faces, skeletons jumped out of the earth beside us with a wild rattle of bones. The dame shrieked, clutched me excitedly. There were moans and groans, wild, grotesque forms that swooped at us from the darkness. Then, with a woosh, a powerful jet of air spurted upwards from the floor of the car.

The dame shrieked as her skirt billowed around her face. The jet continued to play remorselessly. 'My skirt,' she squealed, breathlessly.

Through the darkness I could sense it fluttering. I reached

out, grabbed it, smoothed it down across her thighs. I made one mistake. At the last moment, the powerful air jet whisked the frock from my fingers. I wasn't smoothing anything across her thighs except her skin.

She let loose a coupla more shrieks. They were different from the others, shrieks that were outraged and shocked.

'Gee, I'm sorry,' I apologised.

Her palm cracked against my cheek.

'Hey,' I protested.

The wind cut off abruptly, we spun into a lighted section of the tunnel, coloured waterfalls on either side.

'You shouldn't have taken advantage of me like that,' she flared indignantly.

'I was trying to help,' I protested. 'I was trying to pull down your skirt, and …'

She thawed far too eagerly. 'Oh, were you really? I thought you were being horrible.' She flashed me sheep's eyes. 'I'm so sorry. You will forgive me, won't you?'

'Of course,' I muttered. I was realising what a sap I'd been. It had been a first-class opportunity to shelve her. Instead of which, she was snuggling more closely to me as we once again entered a darkened section of tunnel.

I sat stiff as a ramrod through the rest of the tunnel. I could sense the disappointment inside her. She was a prim and proper dame. But she hadn't wiped arm-squeezing or maybe cuddling off her slate.

'I've offended you,' she pouted as we glided to a standstill at the starting point.

I looked around anxiously. The three kids had given up, had disappeared completely. 'That's okay,' I grunted. 'You weren't to know.'

She took my arm, held it tightly. 'It's curious, the way life is,' she said dreamily. 'If I hadn't been here tonight and you hadn't been here, we might never have met.'

There was no denying the logic of her statement. But it didn't alter my problem. I'd ditched the three kids. Now I had an ugly duckling on my hands.

Okay. I'll admit it. I'm a heel. She was a nice-natured dame, friendly, kindly and very human. Yet I wanted to ditch her, treat her badly on account of just one thing – her face.

I was mean about her. A bigger and better guy wouldn't have wanted to ditch her on that account. He'd have strung along with her on account of her pleasant nature. But I've gotta be honest. I couldn't be happy stringing along with a dame when every time I look at her I'm trying not to. You have to be what you are. I tried to be big, told myself good looks didn't mean a thing. It didn't work. Every time I looked at her, saw that large wart, I was mentally wielding a surgeon's scalpel, cutting it away. I couldn't act normal with her. She was getting buoyed up and excited now, trying to consolidate the progress she had made. It was odds on I was the first guy who had kissed her in a long time. Romance had come into her life with a surge. She was getting coquettish. Can you imagine? Coquettish – with a wart!

She clung like a limpet, hugged my arm, told me all about herself. I was moody, glum, wondering how I could shelve her. We came to a booth where a guy with a megaphone was rallying an audience for the event of the evening.

'Let's see what this is,' I suggested.

The booth was getting a lotta attention. At the back was a large displayed notice that read: *Everybody wins a prize.* Underneath in smaller lettering were the words: *Half the proceeds are for charity.*

The barker stood on a high platform. In front of him, seated on a chair, was one of the most attractive girls I'd seen in a long time. She was maybe 24 or 25, fair, smooth-skinned and with an almost aristocratic contemptuous curve to her eyebrows. Sitting on that platform in front of the barker she achieved the impossible: she looked beautiful and dignified while at the same time you knew she was warm and friendly.

I particularly liked her blouse. It was of yellow satin with puffed sleeves and drawn close-up around her neck by a silken cord. Satin is shiny, clinging material. This yellow blouse was shining and clinging to a hypnotising extent, outlining cleanly the hard thrust of firm breasts. Just to see her sitting there took my breath away. Her skirt was black and full-length. She wore it long on account of sitting on a high platform, I guess.

The barker bellowed: 'The most unusual and remarkable lottery ever witnessed. Everybody wins a prize.' His hand waved grandly toward an array of prizes, ranging from gleaming coffee spoons to enormous teddy-bears. 'And remember, my friends, half the proceeds go to charity. Take part in this lottery, do yourself a good turn, and at the same time help those not so fortunate as yourselves.'

He paused, took a deep breath. The girl seated in front of him half-turned, smiled up at him. It was a wonderful smile. He smiled back. 'Are you ready, my dear?'

She nodded, said clearly, 'I'm ready.'

He made a great play of it. 'Ladeees and gentlemen,' he roared. 'Please watch me closely.' He snapped his fingers to a male assistant, who handed him a silver tray loaded with folded pieces of paper.

'All you do is choose a number,' roared the barker. Without looking, he reached out to the tray, selected a wadded piece of paper, opened it slowly and with a great flourish. 'Number 23,' he announced loudly.

'Number 23,' echoed the assistant, at the same time consulting the prize display. 'Number 23 wins a teddy-bear,' he announced triumphantly.

'As easy as that,' roared the barker. 'A prize for every ticket. You just can't lose, folks.' He shot his cuffs dramatically, held his arms poised and said, 'Now watch closely, folks.'

He stood alongside the fair girl. 'Are you ready, my dear?'

She smiled, nodded quietly, sat with her hands demurely in her lap.

'Watch me closely, folks,' he roared again.

Everybody was watching him. Curiosity was aroused. *My* curiosity was aroused. The barker reached out, tugged on the silken neck-cord until it came loose. Then, with gentle fingers, he widened the neckline of the blouse. The blouse didn't widen much. But the gentle way he did it made me acutely conscious of firm, warm flesh thrusting against the blouse. It musta affected other folks that way, too. The audience was deadly silent, awe-stricken.

'And now,' said the barker, 'we place the lottery tickets in the container. He reached toward the tray, grabbed a fistful of numbered tickets, pulled on the neckline so it widened to the maximum and dropped the handful of tickets inside her blouse.

There was a kinda suppressed gasp from all over. As he reached for another handful, the girl smiled around charmingly, gently shook the blouse. Through the fine material you could see the wadded up lottery tickets tumbling down between her breasts, heaping up around her waist, where a patent-leather belt tightly drew in the hem of the blouse.

The dame pulled at my arm. 'Let's go,' she said. 'I don't like this.'

'Wait a minute,' I grunted resentfully. 'I wanna see.'

The barker thrust handfuls of lottery tickets down the blouse until the tray was empty. The girl kept shaking the blouse so the tickets fell down around her waist. There was a wad of them clearly outlined through the satin blouse.

Folk were wondering what the next move was gonna be. I thought I knew what it was. But I couldn't believe it. I couldn't believe it, even when the barker announced it.

'Here you are, ladies and gentlemen. Especially the gentlemen! A lottery. The most unusual lottery in the world. Choose your lottery ticket from one of the most delightful lottery boxes ever devised by the mind of man. Every ticket wins a prize. Now, step up lively, folks. Step up real lively. Win yourself a prize. Lottery tickets at a dollar a time, always win you a prize. Step right up smartly. That's the idea, sir. Step right up smartly.'

A dollar was a fantastic price to charge for a lottery ticket. Yet judging from the alacrity with which a number of guys started to climb the platform, a dollar was considered cheap in some circles. What the barker said was true. It was one of the most delightful lottery containers ever devised.

There were ten or twelve guys lined up already. The barker

was getting it organised, one flight of steps up to the platform and the other flight down. He glanced around quickly, calculatingly. Most of the fellas were eager-eyed and excited. Dames in the audience wore shocked and tense expressions. Guys with dolls were finding their arms being tugged. My arm was being tugged.

'I don't like this,' she snapped. 'Let's get out of here.'

'I like it,' I said. 'I want to see what happens.'

'It's disgusting,' she snapped. 'The police ought to do something about it. Why are they standing there doing nothing?'

I followed the direction of her eyes. Yeah, there were a coupla cops on duty. They looked bored and uninterested. Almost as though they knew something the audience didn't.

'Okay, folks,' roared the barker. 'Who's the first lucky gent to take the lucky dip?'

The first fella mounted the platform, handed a dollar bill to the waiting assistant, smiled at the girl as she smiled at him. He stood behind her chair where the barker directed.

'Okay, sir,' said the barker. 'Now just thrust your hand over her right shoulder, dip and see how lucky you can be.'

The girl sat with hands in lap, an almost angelic smile on her face, as the guy sheepishly thrust his hand over her shoulder. Being careful not to obstruct the view of the audience, the barker obligingly pulled on the neckline. The guy hesitated, smiled embarrassedly. The crowd roared encouragement. He grinned some more, drew back his arm and rolled up his sleeve to the elbow. The crowd rocked with laughter.

Next time when the guy put his hand over her shoulder he didn't hesitate. His hand glided in the open neckline, moved slowly downwards.

That blouse being satin, you couldn't miss what was happening. You could see his fingers moving beneath the soft material and you could see her. He dipped slowly and lingeringly. One moment there was surprise in his eyes and then a happy grin. His hand moved embracingly, and the crowd roared. The dame tensed like she was being tickled, then giggled, doubled herself over, clutching at herself and his hands protectively.

The barker, grinning broadly, tapped him on the shoulder. 'Plenty more waiting, fella. Don't hog her. Grab your ticket and scram.'

The guy grinned sheepishly when he withdrew the ticket. He got a prize, right enough. An ornamented teaspoon. He could have got ten for his dollar.

The girl straightened up, placed her hands demurely in her lap, and smiled sweetly at the next guy. He dipped with a swift, experienced circling movement. After moments of tensing herself, the girl once again doubled up with a fit of the giggles. The second guy forgot what he was after. He came up without the lottery ticket. By that time, the third guy was ready and waiting, his sleeve rolled up and a grin of anticipation on his face.

The dame tugged on my arm. 'It's absolutely disgusting,' she announced, bridling with indignation and anger. 'How can a woman dare to have the effrontery in front of all these people? And to think of those policemen ...'

'Wait a minute,' I growled. 'I'm interested. I want to see what happens.'

She stared at me. She said in a shocked voice. 'I believe you'd go up there yourself, pay a dollar to ...' she stuttered, unable to finish her sentence.

I knew instinctively this was the moment to ditch her. 'What if I do pay a dollar?' I demanded.

'You wouldn't,' she protested. 'You couldn't!'

'And supposin' I do?'

'I wouldn't stay long enough to watch,' she flared. She was trembling with indignation.

'Lady,' I said grimly, 'you can start getting ready to walk out on me.'

I shouldered my way toward the line of waiting men. There were a coupla dozen of them now. She followed after me a coupla paces and then stopped irresolutely. I stared at her challengingly. She stared back, equally challengingly. The queue was moving quickly. In no time at all, there were only twelve to go. And then nine. Then I was halfway up the steps leading to the platform.

The dame and her wart were both watching me. I knew she meant what she said. She was outraged. The moment I paid my dollar, she'd stalk away contemptuously.

That was maybe the best way for it to finish.

The guy next to me moved on, the barker's assistant grinned, held out his hand. 'That'll be a buck, mister.'

I handed him a buck, glanced in the direction of the wart. Her shoulders were contemptuous, her head high and proud as she stalked away from me. That red blouse and black skirt still looked good from behind.

'Hurry up there, fella,' growled the barker. 'Ain't you anxious?' He raised his voice to the crowd. 'Here's a guy that ain't so anxious!'

I stepped up behind the girl. She smiled at me. It was a nice smile. And all at once I became twenty times more conscious of the graceful firmness of her body beneath that satin blouse. Up there, close up, I could see her twenty times more clearly. Unaccountably, my mouth was dry and my breath short. My fingers were tingling with anticipation as I stood behind her, slipped my hand over her shoulder and dipped into the neckline obligingly held open by the barker.

I wasn't any more interested in a lottery ticket than the other guys. It was exquisitely, femininely rounded, firmly sculptured and distinctively shaped. I did what all the other guys had done, grinned and explored extravagantly, until she giggled, doubled herself up, as though I'd tickled her unbearably. I even remembered to draw out a ticket. As I did so, I said softly in her ear, 'I'd like to try that again, honey. But some other time, some other place.'

She gave me a second glance, missed smiling at the guy next to me. It was a swift, searching glance, as though she wanted to memorise me, know me again.

That was all. I collected my teaspoon, tucked it into my coat pocket and went down the stairs the other side of the platform.

There were a couple of college kids standing there, watching with eager, excited eyes. One of them caught my arm. 'Say, mister,' he asked breathlessly. 'How is it? A good dollar's worth?'

I suppressed a grin. 'How did it look?'

'Gee,' he said, in hushed, reverent tones. 'It looked real good.'

'It's just the same as it looks,' I told him, and strolled on.

College kids, like everyone else, should pay for experience. Why should I tell him? Let him find out for himself.

Anyone should have known from the way the cops stood around with bored, uninterested looks on their faces that the girl was safe. Yeah, she was safe. Yeah, sitting up there on that platform with a dozen guys a minute plunging their arms down her neckline she was as safe as though they weren't in the same room as her.

You couldn't touch that girl. You literally couldn't touch her. It was beautifully made, probably of copper. It began immediately below the neckline and extended to her waist, the most ingenious cheater ever invented in this modern age. Ingenious, I say, because most cheaters merely cheat. This one cheated and earned a dollar a time in addition.

I sighed. I hadn't had a promising start to my vacation. On the run from three determined teenagers, my face smacked by a dame I couldn't bear to look at and the final humiliation of being taken for a sucker at a fairground.

Yeah, I've gotta be honest about it. It wasn't only to get rid of the wart I bought that lottery ticket.

2

It was hot the following morning. The sun got up early, blazed fiercely out of a blue sky. It was the kinda morning you feel good to be alive.

I ate breakfast on the veranda, sat in the comfortable shade wearing white ducks[2], staring across the white sands at the warm blue sea, which tumbled playfully up the beach in a flurry of white foam.

It was a beautiful day, it was a beautiful position. There was only one thing wrong with it. People!

There weren't a lot of them. But there were too many. They sat themselves on the sands, erected their big, gaily-coloured umbrellas. A party parked themselves right in front of me, midway between my veranda and the sea. They were a nice enough bunch of folks, a family and children out for the day. But they irritated me. I liked solitude. I liked to bask in the sun with only the sound of the waves in my ears, to swim leisurely and alone, to wade from the sea glistening with water and run powerfully across the soft white sand, turn cartwheels and enjoy the glow of wellbeing induced by physical health.

On arrival in Long View Beach I'd hired a car. It was a cream

---

[2] Editor's note: a term commonly used in the 1950s for men's light casual trousers.

coupe, sports model, ideal as a runabout. I rolled my bathing trunks in a towel, told the coloured cook I'd be back at one o'clock for lunch and tooled the coupe from the garage.

I took the coast road, followed the beach. My hunch was right. I hadn't far to go before I found deserted stretches of beach.

I drove on. I wanted to find the right spot, the kind of place that I could go to every day, that I could make specifically my own.

I found that, too. A small bay, quiet and secluded, white sands against the blue sea and a clump of flowering palm trees to give it the final touch of South Sea Island solitude.

There was a short climb down to the beach. I stopped the car on the main coast road, changed into my bathing costume, locked my clothes in the car and slithered down to the beach.

It was hot now, really hot. I could feel the rays of the sun probing into me, burning my skin, tanning it thoroughly and charging me with life-giving vigour. I went right to the water's edge, lay out on the gently-shelving sands within reach of the surf. It was so peaceful there I wouldn't have changed places with anyone else in the world. You can imagine it, the sun warming my body, charging it with energy and vigour as an accumulator is charged. Every wave that broke against the beach sent white foam swirling up and around me, an automatic cooling process.

I could have lain that way forever. There was a rhythm to the wash of that surf that made me sleepy. The roar of a breaker hitting the beach, the soft swish of water across sand, the cool touch of it as it swirled around me, and then the swish of thousands and thousands of tiny fragments of sand whispering against each other as they were sucked back toward the sea.

It was the slamming of a car door that roused me. It carried clearly on the still air. I swore softly to myself, squirmed around on my belly and looked up toward the road. A long, expensive-looking saloon car had pulled up behind mine. Two guys had climbed out of it and were conferring excitedly. They didn't seem to notice me. They came to agreement, split up, and each took a path that led out to one of the two spurs that formed the bay.

I watched them as each reached the end of his spur, settled down and lit a cigarette. The one on my right could see the beach the other side of the bay that I couldn't. He signalled to his companion, who waved his hand in understanding.

There was a queer, fluttery feeling deep down in my belly. The kinda feeling I get when something isn't right. These two guys were lying in wait for somebody. They were gonna trap them. What was more, they were in a perfect position to trap them. Anyone coming along the beach would have to pass the spur on the right of the bay, where there was only a narrow strip of sand between the tip of the spur and the sea. Once the victim entered the bay, the guy on the spur could quickly slither down the rocks and cut off his retreat. The guy at the other side of the bay could prevent escape at that point.

I sat up quickly. My sudden movement was noticed by both of them. At that distance I couldn't see their faces, but the way they suddenly froze showed I'd surprised them.

I stood up, waded out into the water. When it was chest-high, I looked along the beach. I could see beyond the spur now. I could see who they were waiting for: a black-haired dame wearing a blood-red frock. She was half-running, half-walking, white sand spurting like smoke from her heels.

Maybe I was imagining things. I was so used to looking for trouble that I sometimes tried to find it where none existed. This was a holiday beach in Florida. Why should I be looking for trouble? Why should there be any?

I waded out from the sea, sat on the sand and let the sun dry me. From time to time I looked up, glanced toward the spur on my right. She came around it, still half-running, half-walking. She was staring straight ahead of her like she could see only the place she was making for, in such a hurry and that nothing else mattered. The guy on the spur waited until she was halfway toward me then swiftly clambered down the rocks to the beach. He followed the dame, carefully, cautiously, like a lion stalking its prey. I felt the hairs on the back of my neck bristle. I got up slowly, determinedly.

She was almost level with me now, so I got a good look at her. She was beautiful, her face an aesthetic white oval against the rich blackness of her thick, shoulder-length hair. Her red frock was a brilliant slash of colour against the white sands, drawn tight at bodice and waist, but with a full skirt that billowed around her thighs.

She didn't look at me, acted like she didn't know I was there. When she was close, I said quietly, 'Listen, lady. If you're in any kinda trouble, you can always call on me.' She stumbled past blindly, eyes staring into the far distance like she could see an objective that had to be achieved at all costs.

I stood staring after her, blankly. She was almost at the tip of the other spur when the second man appeared. He'd climbed down around the far side, got around in front of her.

She might have been blind to me. But she wasn't blind to this guy. As he materialised in front of her she stopped dead, tensed all over like she was bracing herself to resist him. Then she spun around, came running back toward me, toward the other guy following her, who was nearly level with me.

She wasn't blind to him either. Once again she stopped dead, looked desperately to left and right.

I tensed, flexed my muscles. The guy nearest me rasped loudly, 'Hold it, fella. You don't want to get mixed up in this.'

I eyed him carefully, weighed him up. He was a big guy, broad and muscular. His battered features showed he'd spent time inside the ropes.

'What goes on?' I demanded. 'Just leave the dame alone.'

He worked his face into an ugly grin. His blue eyes smiled disarmingly. 'A little domestic trouble, fella,' he said gently. 'The dame's my sister. The guy is her husband. They've been having one of their quarrels.'

I shot a quick look at the dame. She was running toward the road now, running desperately like her life depended on it. The other guy was right behind her, reaching out to grab her shoulder. Even as I glanced toward her she stumbled. The guy behind was swift, launched himself at her, arms encircling her waist so that they fell together, the dame kicking and fighting madly to get free.

I didn't hesitate. I ran over to them. At least, I intended to.

I should have remembered the other guy. He was thinking way ahead of me, had calculated exactly what I'd do. When I burst into a run, I succeeded only in sprawling on my face. He'd sidled up close, looped his foot around in front of my ankles.

My eyes and mouth were full of sand as I levered my chest upwards. He jumped on me. The painful, gouging impact of his boot heels between my shoulder-blades slammed my chest against the sand, drove the breath from my lungs.

Instinctively I rolled to avoid his boots as they smashed down for the second time. But he was outthinking me all the time. He anticipated so well that his boot was already swinging as I rolled my unprotected belly within range.

I jack-knifed, gasped with breathless agony. There was a ringing in my ears, and the sky and the sand were the same shade of pain-wracked grey through which the pink blob of his battered features loomed close.

'You shoulda kept outta this, bud. It's a domestic matter, see?'

His voice echoed from the end of a long black tunnel. So did the meaty clump of knuckles against flesh. The ache of my jaw was living inside me, reducing the black tunnel to a pinpoint that disappeared into nothingness as he uppercut me a second time.

* * *

The coolness of water splashing on my face brought me around. I opened my eyes, blinked painfully as salt water stung painfully, and stared up into an anxious face that was vaguely familiar.

'How d'you feel?' she asked anxiously.

I remembered everything in a flash, as though I'd never been unconscious. 'Those damned swine,' I growled, and then winced with the sudden ache of my jaw.

'Lie quietly,' she said. 'Don't talk.'

I resisted her detaining hands, levered myself up on my elbows, glanced around. The men were gone. So was the dame. So was the long black saloon!

'What was it about?' she asked.

I climbed to my feet unsteadily, glared around impotently. There was an agonising imprint of boot heels between my shoulder-blades, my belly was raw and tender, bleeding where a toe-cap had scraped skin, my jaw was swollen to twice its normal size and every tooth in my head ached. I was burning, mad to get my hands on somebody, tear them apart.

'What was it about?' she repeated. 'How did it start?'

'You go tell the cops,' I rasped abruptly. 'A dame's been kidnapped.' I stared at her thoughtfully. 'Say, how much of it did you see? You saw the dame?'

She shook her head slowly, her eyes saying that she thought I was just a little crazy. She looked familiar. Someplace quite recently I'd seen her, spoken to her.

'I was walking along the beach,' she said. 'I saw you and another man struggling. I saw him kick you.' She shuddered. 'I ran all the way here, but he'd disappeared by the time I arrived.'

'There was a dame,' I said thickly. 'And there were two men. They musta kidnapped the dame.'

There was worry in her eyes. 'Maybe you oughta sit down,' she said. 'The sun's hot and you've been knocked out. You oughta take things easy.'

'Look,' I glared. 'When I start imagining things …' I broke off, stared at her really hard, licked my lips. 'Now I've got it!' I said triumphantly.

'Got what?'

'You're the lottery dame,' I burst out. 'The iron-chested girl.'

She flushed, dropped her eyes.

I dropped my eyes, too. Dropped them low enough to check her credentials. She was wearing a one-piece sea-green bathing costume that looked like it was made of silk. Her bathing-wrap was slung carelessly around her shoulders, concealing nothing.

I took a deep breath, whistled my admiration. Her blue eyes

looked up sharply. She blushed even more when she saw where I was looking, the way I was looking!

She stood her ground, defiantly and challengingly, her cheeks stained red. After a long pause she demanded, 'Well?'

'Very, very nice,' I said approvingly.

Her lip curled. 'You're the type of man that infuriates me,' she said contemptuously.

I grinned. 'Because I'm looking at you?'

'Because you're looking that way,' she snapped.

'Don't give me that,' I drawled. 'You could wear a thick woollen costume like grandmother wore, fitting tight around ankles and wrists. But you don't. You're wearing little more than a pocket handkerchief, as thin as silk and stretched tight as a drum. You do that for only one reason, baby. So that guys like me will look at you.'

Her blue eyes flashed angrily, she half-pulled the wrap around in front of her. It didn't help cover her. I eyed her appreciatively. 'Tell me, babe? Is it the cheater or is it really you?'

'I remember you now,' she said accusingly. Her eyes narrowed. 'You're the one who spoke to me.'

'I remember you,' I said. 'The way I figure it, you owe me a dollar.'

She said levelly, 'You're just about the most unbearable man I've ever met, and …'

A sudden stab of pain in my aching jaw made me wince. It also made me think of other things. 'That dame,' I muttered. 'We've gotta do something about that dame.'

Her blue eyes weighed me up. 'You sure took a nasty crack,' she commented.

'They had a car,' I said, with a worried frown. 'You'd better contact the cops, have it put on the air.'

She said quietly, 'It's a touch of the sun. Lots of folks get it here.'

I glared at her. I said slowly and deliberately, 'There were two guys and a dame. That dame was kidnapped, taken off in a long black saloon.'

'You're dreaming,' she said. 'You were knocked unconscious. How could you see all that?'

'I saw the two guys and the dame,' I protested. 'I saw one of them struggling with the dame.'

'I saw only one man,' she said levelly. 'It looked like he had a grudge against you.'

I rubbed my jaw. 'I'd like to meet up with him,' I said darkly.

'What was it about?' she asked. 'Why did he do it?'

I glared at her angrily. 'Because I was trying to …'

'… save the girl from being kidnapped,' she interrupted mockingly.

I glared at her ferociously. 'You don't have to believe me,' I growled. 'What do I care what you think?'

She shrugged her shoulders. 'It's nothing to do with me. If you wanna tell a crazy story like that to the cops, stir up a hornets' nest around your ears, that's your business.'

'Yeah,' I flared. 'It's my business.'

I stalked away from her, strode across the sand toward my car. But as the car got nearer my steps got slower. There was a lot in what she said. As a witness, she was no help. All she'd seen was one guy belting me. And how did I know the dame was being kidnapped anyway? The guy had said it was a domestic affair.

I was supposed to be on holiday. I'd look a sucker being involved in a charge of obstructing the police by giving false information. What had I to go on anyway? Just a hunch!

I turned around, went back to the girl. She'd dropped her wrap, was standing gracefully with her face lifted toward the sun, drinking it in. I came up alongside her, stood there drinking *her* in.

'Thought better of it?' she asked.

'Yeah,' I said drily. 'I've thought better of it.' My mouth was dry, and I couldn't take my eyes off her. I'd thought the satin blouse at that lottery was revealing; but this costume looked like it was painted on her.

'If you want to make a complaint about the man who attacked you, I'll give evidence,' she said.

'The only thing wrong with that suggestion,' I gritted, 'is that I don't know him. Never seen him before.'

She shot me a quick glance. 'Why did he do it then?'

I sighed. 'Don't let's go into that again. Let's talk about something pleasant. About you, for example.' I grinned. 'You didn't answer my question. Is it the cheater? Or is it the real you?'

She flushed, but there was a sparkle of flattered vanity in her eyes. 'It's me, of course.' Then she chided gently, 'You really shouldn't be asking intimate questions like that.'

'You know something,' I said. 'When I first saw you sitting on that platform, I decided it was too good to be true. After I'd paid my dollar, I discovered it *was* too good to be true. Now I'm back where I started, still wondering and hoping.'

'Why?' she asked sweetly. She knew why, but she wanted to hear me say it.

'It still looks too good to be true.'

She blushed shyly. 'The cheater's handmade, made to measure,' she confessed. 'This is really me.'

'The cheater must be a perfect fit. Maybe I can check the measurements sometime?'

Her lips pursed primly. 'I've been very lenient with you. But you go too far! Excuse me.'

She ran into the surf, took a low, neat dive. She didn't invite me, but I didn't need an invitation. I went after her. She could swim like a fish. She cut through the water easily and swiftly like an eel. I only ever got close enough to have water splashed in my face and hear her mocking laughter as she slipped out of reach.

She got out of the water ahead of me, laughing and shaking the water from her hair with a pretty toss of her head. She dried herself deftly with the bath-wrap, grinned at me impishly as I waded out of the water, breathing hard.

'Let me do that for you,' I offered.

'Oh, no!' she grinned warily, skipping a couple of paces beyond my reach.

'You know something?'

'I ought to, at my age.'

'You're cute,' I said. 'Real cute.'

She narrowed her eyes artfully, looked through her eyelashes. 'You're not so bad yourself.'

I moved in a couple of paces. She skipped back a couple of paces, giggled. 'From a distance,' she added.

I scowled sulkily. 'Get this straight,' I growled. 'I ain't chasin' you.'

'That's fine,' she said. 'That's just the way I like it. I wouldn't ever feel safe with you around, unless you were handcuffed.'

I scowled some more. She had the kinda shape you see only in dreams, and she was showing all of it. She knew what it was doing to me; but every time I made a tentative move toward her, she slapped me down. She handed me every inducement to make a pass and criticised when I did. She was playing with me.

'You're okay,' I sneered. 'I wouldn't make a pass even if you paid me a dollar.'

Her eyes were offended and annoyed. But she was too proud to show it. She carried it off with a rippling little laugh. 'In that case, everything's fine, because I wouldn't pay you a dollar even if I had one.'

'That's fine with me, too,' I growled, trying not to notice she'd skilfully come almost within reach, tantalisingly ready to slip quickly away.

'The swim was marvellous,' she said appreciatively 'It's given me an appetite. I feel I could eat a horse.'

The sun was so hot I was already dry, the salt from the water crystallising on the hairs on my arms. I realised the pain in my belly wasn't all caused by the kick I'd received. I was hungry too.

'Where d'you eat?' I asked.

'At home.'

'Where's home?'

She pointed along the beach, miles back toward the fairground.

'Justa minute,' I said. 'How did you get here?'

'Walked,' she said simply.

I stared at her. 'It must be all of five miles.'

She nodded, smiled charmingly. 'Almost six,' she corrected. 'But I like swimming alone. The beach is too crowded that end. Besides, walking's good for my figure.' She moved herself subtly, as though to say: *See what good shape walking keeps me in?*

I gulped, looked into her blue eyes instead of at her subtly weaving hips. 'You're not walking back?' I said incredulously.

She nodded. 'I always do.'

'Let me drop you,' I suggested. 'It'll take a coupla hours to walk back. You'll be famished by then.'

She looked back along the beach as though calculating the distance. Then she looked at me thoughtfully. 'It's kind of you to offer,' she said. 'I'd like to accept … on one condition.'

'What's that?'

'No passes.'

I scowled. 'What do you figure you're made of, tissue paper?'

She smiled impishly. 'I'm just a cautious girl. No passes?'

'No passes,' I grunted.

We climbed up to my car. It was a tricky climb and she had to give me her hand so I could help her. Her fingers were cool, her skin soft. I wanted to run the tips of my fingers along her arm; but I fought the impulse, wouldn't let myself give way.

She waited with face averted while I climbed into the car, changed into my white ducks. Then she climbed in, sat next to me with the white wrap around her shoulders and her shapely thighs constantly in the corner of my eye.

'What's your name?' I asked.

'Jane,' she said. 'Jane Langley.'

'I'm Hank,' I said. 'Hank Janson.'

'I think you'll reverse the car better if you watch where you're going instead of my legs.'

'I'm doing fine,' I grunted.

I got the car turned around, headed back toward town. After a few moments she asked, 'Got a cigarette.'

'In my jacket pocket, the one nearest to you.'

She leaned over, fumbled in my pocket. She took a cigarette for herself, pushed one between my lips; she fumbled again, found the matches. She lit her own cigarette first, leaned against me so that she could hold the end of her cigarette to mine. Her shoulder touched mine, her bare knee touched my thigh.

'Hey!' I said.

'Want something?' she drawled huskily.

'Yeah,' I said. 'Stop making passes.'

She glared at me angrily, guiltily. Then sulkily she pushed herself away from me, sat with a wide gap between us, and her forehead creased in a pretty frown.

'I wouldn't feel safe with you around unless you had your hands handcuffed,' I growled.

She glared at me. There were hard glints in her blue eyes. Then gradually her face softened, her lips twitched and she chuckled softly. 'Okay, Hank,' she admitted. 'I've been beastly. It's an imp of mischief inside me. I like getting attention. Just can't help myself.'

I grinned too. 'The next time I make a pass, you'd better accept it.'

She said quietly, seriously. 'There won't be a next time, Hank. I don't want you making any real passes. So I won't invite them again.'

3

Jane lived in a middle-class boarding house. I tried to date her up. She thanked me for the lift, said smilingly she'd see me sometime.

I sighed. The first really interesting dame I'd hit up against in Florida and she was playing hard to get.

My coloured woman cooked good. I dozed for an hour after lunch, and because there was nothing else to do, took a book and my bathing trunks and drove back to the bay where I'd swum that morning.

I'd been lying in the shade of the palm tree for about an hour when my solitude was disturbed. He was an erect old guy, maybe 60 years of age with iron grey hair and a waxed, pointed moustache. He wore white ducks, a large white, floppy-brimmed Panama and white shoes.

He came right over to me, stared down with hard blue eyes. 'Nice day, son,' he said.

I propped myself up on one elbow. 'Yeah,' I agreed. 'That's one thing this place is good for. The weather!'

He took off his Panama, wiped the sweat from his forehead with a white silk handkerchief. I looked him over closely, noticed his clothes were expensive, his shirt embroidered with his initials, and the wristwatch on his lean brown arm was made of platinum.

'Mind if I join you, son?'

He sat down beside me easily and lithely like a boy. He had

a good, strong face, eyes that were searching and honest. He drew a gold, engraved case from his pocket, opened it, offered me a cigar.

'Well, if you can spare it …' I began.

'Sure, sure,' he said. He rammed the case under my nose.

We lit up in appreciative silence. They were good cigars. Life seemed sweet at that moment, the pleasant tang of the cigar in my nostrils, the soft wash of the surf on the beach and the pleasant shade from the palm tree.

'Had a nasty bang on the chin, haven't you, son?'

I fingered my jaw, grinned ruefully. 'Yeah, had a little trouble this morning.'

The blue eyes were searching, compelling. I had an overwhelming impulse to tell him everything. When I was through talking, I was surprised at myself. Yet at the same time I wasn't surprised. He was the kind of guy who invited confidences.

He stared at me solemnly. 'Why didn't you tell the police?' he asked.

'What could I tell them?' I said. 'It coulda been a kidnapping. But it's unlikely. I'd have maybe stirred up mud for nothing.'

He thought about it. He said finally, 'I think you did the right thing, son.'

'But I'm plenty worried,' I told him. 'If there's so much as a whisper that a dame's missing, I'll feel as guilty as hell.'

'I shouldn't worry about it, son. Like the fella said, it's probably a domestic matter.' He drew on his cigar, asked casually, 'On holiday here?'

'A few weeks,' I told him.

'Come from hereabouts?'

'Chicago.'

'City man, huh?' There was interest in his voice. 'Salesman or something?'

'Reporter,' I corrected.

We were there talking for maybe a coupla hours. He was a guy named Rawlins. He owned a big house a coupla miles farther on. Piecing together scraps of information, I realised he must be loaded with dough. He casually mentioned a coupla oil-wells he owned in Texas and a steel works in Detroit. His wife had died a few years earlier. He and his daughter lived alone, except for the servants.

'You must come up to the house sometime, son,' he invited.

'I'd like to.'

'Drop in anytime. You'll always be welcome.'

The cool of the evening was setting in when he got up, flexed his muscles, nodded and walked away with that upright, athletic, almost military stride.

I watched until he was out of sight the other side of the spur and then ran down to the sea, plunged in. I luxuriated in the water a long time. Then I called it a day, went to my car and drove slowly back to the villa, where early dinner was being prepared.

The pattern of holiday life was already forming. Mornings and afternoons lounging in the sun in the bay, and the evenings … yeah, the evenings!

It's fine to take a walk on a warm, quiet night when the moon's shining brightly. Yeah, it's real fine. But it's a hundred times better if you're not alone. And everybody, it seemed, was attracted to the bright lights of the fairground.

I fought against it for a long while, but that's where my feet were finally taking me. It was late then, some of the booths already beginning to close. As though magnetised, there was only one place in that fairground to which I was drawn.

She was up there on the platform, still sitting with her hands demurely in her lap. This booth was closing too, the last dozen fellas lined up and the assistant heading off the others.

I watched with mingled feelings. It was fun to see the anticipation on those guys' faces and know the disappointment they were gonna suffer. But every time a guy stepped up behind her, reached out like he'd bought her, it made me boil. I couldn't figure how a nice dame like her could sit hour after hour, switching on a sweet smile and giggling coquettishly at the psychological moment.

There was overwhelming relief inside me when the barker

stepped forward, announced loudly, 'That's all for tonight, folks. Tell your friends to come along tomorrow and win a prize.'

The girl stepped off the platform, went into a tent at the back. The barker followed her, and the crowd began to drift away. Maybe it was my loneliness, or maybe I was remembering the way she'd looked that morning in that tight swimming costume, but I hung around the booth, and was surprised when she came out quickly. It had taken her no time at all to change into a crisp white blouse and black skirt. I stepped in front of her and she drew back in startled surprise, quickly smiling and relaxing as she recognised me. 'You startled me.'

'If you're not doing anything special, I could show you the sights,' I offered.

'You can walk me home, if you like.'

'You don't fancy a long walk in the moonlight?'

She looked at me solemnly. 'Just to my home.'

I shrugged. 'I'll take an option on that if there's nothing else on offer.'

She fell into step beside me. 'I'm not very romantic, am I?'

I scowled. 'You don't act easy to get,' I said. 'That's why I don't understand a nice dame like you in a sex racket, shearing the suckers at a dollar a time.'

'It's for charity,' she said.

'Those guys aren't interested in charity,' I said bitterly. 'They're interested in you. And either way, they don't get what they want.'

She was quiet, a shadow slipped across her face. 'The money's good,' she said. 'That's what counts.'

'You could earn less and live better.'

Her voice was cold and controlled. 'You can leave me to be the judge of that.'

'Keep your hair pinned up,' I said. 'I was getting it off my chest.'

'We're almost home now,' she said. 'There's no need for you to come to the door.'

'I can stagger a few more paces.'

It was late, the street-lighting was dim, and there was nobody around. I went up the steps with her, waited on the porch while she fumbled in her handbag. It was shadowy there, so her face was a white blur.

'Nice of you to see me home,' she said. 'Thanks a lot.'

'Look,' I said. 'I'm lonely.'

There was a long pause. 'I'm sorry,' she said quietly.

'I'm warning you,' I said levelly. 'I'm gonna make a pass.'

There was an even longer pause. Her voice was emotionless. 'I wish you wouldn't.'

'I can't help myself, honey,' I said huskily. I moved in quickly, slipped my arms around her. I didn't have to search for her lips, they were uptilted, moist and clinging. There was the smell of her perfume in my nostrils and the sweetness of honey on her lips. She pulled herself away, gave a deep sigh of contentment. 'That was a wonderful goodnight kiss, Hank.'

That hadn't been a goodnight kiss. It had only whetted my appetite. I moved in breathlessly, pulled her close. For a moment she was warm and pliant. She realised the same moment as me what was happening. She pushed herself away angrily, slapped my face hard so that my head rocked on my shoulders.

Maybe I deserved having my face smacked. But it was so terribly unjust, because she hadn't discarded the iron chest.

'I'm sorry, Hank,' she said quickly, penitently.

'I'm sorry, too,' I grunted. I kept well away from her now, like she was red hot.

'It was my fault.' There was a kinda charm in her voice. 'I guess I forgot myself for the moment, and then …'

'Sure,' I said bitterly. 'You forgot. You almost became human.'

She was breathless. 'You'd better not see me again, Hank.'

'Don't be scared,' I sneered. 'That's the last pass I'll ever make.'

'I'm sorry,' she said humbly.

There was a long silence. She broke it finally. 'Well, goodbye,

Hank.'

'It was nice knowing you,' I said bitterly.

She pushed the key into the lock, opened the door and slipped inside. There was a kinda choke in her voice as she closed the door behind her, said through it, 'Goodbye, Hank.'

'In confidence,' I rasped, 'do you sleep in that thing as well?'

The door shut in my face.

I was fuming. My cheek still stung. If she hadn't been so responsive at first, if I hadn't sensed it was what she wanted, it would never have happened. I mentally resolved she had encouraged me to the point where she could slap me down for the last time.

I drove back to my villa angrily, stumped along the path and clumped up the veranda steps. It was in darkness, and I was startled when a dimly-seen white-clad figure seated comfortably in a cane chair greeted me: 'Hiya, son.'

I silenced the defensive flutter of fear inside me, drew a deep breath and asked suspiciously, 'What are you doing here?'

'Looking for you, son.' A cigarette lighter sparked into flame, a red glow reflected on his face as he drew on a cigar. His honest blue eyes stared at me levelly.

I was sorry I'd spoken so brusquely. I tried to cover up, invited quickly, 'Come on inside. We'll have a drink.'

'Nice idea,' he grunted.

I opened up, switched on the light. He followed me inside, rested his Panama on one chair, settled himself comfortably in another.

'Scotch?' I asked.

'And the same amount of soda water.'

I poured the drinks, got ice cubes from the ice-box and dropped them into the tall glasses. It was a warm evening. We sat opposite each other in the cool cane chairs, cuddled our glasses and watched each other with interest.

'I'll come straight to the point, Janson,' he said.

'Yeah?' I eyed him keenly, wondered what was on his mind.

'I've checked up on you,' he said approvingly. 'From all I've learned, you're the guy I need.'

I got up slowly, put my drink on the table. I said softly and grimly, 'What the hell d'you mean, you've checked up on me!'

The blue eyes flicked up at me, smiled gently. 'Sit down, son,' he said easily. 'Don't blow your top with me. I've a proposition that'll interest you. But I had to be sure of you first, sure of the man I was dealing with.'

I sat down again. I couldn't help it. He was that kinda guy.

'You've got a good record,' he went on. 'You're honest, reliable and a good man to have around in a tight squeeze. That confirms the impression I got when I spoke to you this afternoon.'

'What proposition?' I rasped. 'What's on your mind?'

He studied the end of his cigar. 'I'm a very wealthy man.'

'So's Rockefeller. But he hasn't checked up on me.'

He ignored my interruption, went on talking quietly. 'I've got a daughter. She's ill. She's in a bad way. I figure you can help me with her.'

I stared at him. 'Did you check up on my medical degrees?' I sneered.

He looked at me steadily. 'I'm not joking, Janson,' he said. 'My daughter's ill. I'm convinced you're the man who can help her.'

I swallowed. 'What d'ya mean – ill?'

'Dope,' he said bitterly. Just the way he pronounced that one word revealed all the misery and unhappiness bottled up inside him. I knew at once the trouble, appreciated it and sympathised with him.

'How bad?'

'She's overboard with it. Crazy when she can't get it.'

I spread my hands. 'Where do I come in?'

Blue eyes rested on me levelly. 'Look after her day and night. Keep her away from the dope, somehow.'

I breathed deeply. 'That's a big job,' I said. 'There's hospitals to take care of those cases. They have doctors, a staff of nurses. They have everything on tap. Why don't you do the job properly?'

The blue eyes were still fastened on me. He said slowly,

'She's my daughter, Janson. She's all I've got in the world. You're the type of guy who can keep a grip on his tongue. And that's important. I want to get my daughter over this illness without anyone knowing about it. It's not a pleasant thing to happen to your daughter. I don't want it to get around, have folk pointing at her, talking about her, saying she used to be a dope addict.'

'I appreciate your difficulty,' I said politely. 'But I'm on vacation. I'm due back in a few weeks. And … well, this kinda thing is way off my beat. I'm not a doctor, I'm just a newshawk.'

He leaned forward, clasped his hands together. 'I'm pleading with you, Janson,' he said softly. 'You know as well as I do there's only one way for her to beat the dope. She's gotta lay off drugs for two or three weeks. Allow the effects of them to clear right out of her system. She'll go through hell during that time. Yes, I know all about it, because I've studied it. She'll suffer. She'll suffer terribly. But afterwards, she'll be healthy again. Just two or three weeks, and she'll have got rid of the craving forever.'

'But why me?' I said. 'Why can't you do it?'

His face was haggard now. 'She's my daughter,' he said. 'I couldn't bear to see her suffer that way. I'd break down, give in to her.'

'Okay,' I said. 'Get some guy who doesn't know her, give him strict instructions, let him carry them out.'

'That's what I reckon to do,' he said. 'That's why I'm here. You're the guy I can trust.'

'Look, Mr Rawlins,' I protested. 'I'm not fitted to take on a job like that, and …'

His blue eyes were piercing and searching. 'There's another reason, too, Janson,' he said. 'I've gotta have a good guy. A guy I can trust. When anyone's under the influence of dope, they'll do anything to get more. Anything!'

'I don't get you.'

'Where getting drugs is concerned,' he said slowly, 'moral behaviour is forgotten. The addict will do anything to get further supplies, literally anything!' He added slowly, 'I don't want to place my daughter in the hands of anyone likely to take advantage of her.'

I gulped. 'What makes you think I'm any less human than the next guy?'

He smiled sadly. 'I don't think you are. But you're the kind of man who will keep his word. I don't think you'd let me down.'

There was a long pause. I said, 'It's nice of you to make me this offer, but ...'

'Don't turn it down,' he said quickly. 'Just come up to my house with me. Come up for half an hour. I want you to meet my daughter. You can decide afterwards.'

I stared at him. He stared back. The expression in his blue eyes was a challenge, seeming to say, *You're afraid to come with me.*

I got up. 'Do we use your car, or mine?'

'We'll use mine,' he said.

4

It was a big, stone-built house located on a deserted stretch of the beach. It was a two-storey house, modern style, and seeming to sprawl like a collection of matchboxes.

A stiff-shirted butler opened the door. Rawlins gave him his hat, strode past him without a word. I followed, looking around me with interest. The room was spacious and beautifully furnished.

'I'll show you around later if you're interested,' said Rawlins. 'But I promised to keep you only half an hour.' As he spoke, he was opening doors, leading me through a succession of beautifully-furnished rooms.

'Moira occupies the right wing of the house,' he explained. 'I thought it better to segregate her as far as possible.'

All the time he was talking, he was walking swiftly. The house looked large from outside. It seemed enormous from inside. I followed down a white-walled corridor lined with modern oil-paintings, my footsteps echoing on the waxed parquet flooring. At the end of the corridor was an oak door.

'This is the right wing,' he said. He paused for a moment. His blue eyes were serious. 'I want you to remember one thing. There's a good reason for everything that happens. Remember that.'

He opened the door. I followed through. It was a large, beautifully-furnished living-room. We passed through, opened the door at the far end. This was another large living-room. But this one was occupied.

I stood in the doorway, stared at them with a knot of fury swelling in my belly. They were seated at the table, cigar-smoke writhing upwards to cloud the atmosphere, their eyes staring stupidly at me across the top of their playing cards.

There was a kinda frozen silence. They recognised me and I recognised them. Rawlins stepped close, gripped my wrist tightly. 'Take it easy, Janson,' he said insistently. 'I can explain everything.'

I wrenched my wrist free, clenched my fists into hard knots. The two guys got up quickly, stood defensively, a glint of fear showing in their eyes at the anger written on my face.

Rawlins moved in front of me quickly. His fingers were like steel when he gripped my arms. 'Don't blow your top, Janson,' he said crisply. 'I told you there's a reasonable explanation for everything. Listen to what I've got to say and you can start fighting afterwards if you want.'

His cool, even voice formed clamps to hold down my anger. I kept myself under control, breathed heavily. 'What are these guys doing here?' I demanded.

'They're looking after Moira,' he said.

My head whirled. Suddenly I began to understand everything. 'You mean,' I faltered, 'these guys ...'

'That's right,' he said softly. 'It was Moira you saw this morning. These men were looking after her, stopping her from making contact with certain people.' The way he put the emphasis on the *certain people* told me he meant dope pedlars.

'I'll introduce you,' he said. He nodded toward the fella who'd knocked me unconscious. 'This is Matt,' he said.

Matt looked at me uneasily. 'Hiya,' he said, with a weak grin.

'You and me must have a talk,' I said.

'That's right,' he said, with a sickly grin.

'And this is Tony.'

Tony looked like he'd been Matt's sparring partner. His nose was bent, one ear was ballooned and he flashed four gold teeth. 'You's de guy from de beach,' he said brightly.

I looked at his gold teeth, wondered how hard I'd have to hit to knock them out. 'You've got a memory,' I said.

'How is she?' asked Rawlins, cutting across the dynamite atmosphere.

'She's okay,' growled Matt. 'Haven't had a peep outta her.'

He sounded casual, offhand. The skin on Rawlins' cheekbones tautened. When he looked at me, his eyes seemed to say, *You see the kinda men I've got to rely on.* He actually said, 'Come along and meet Moira.'

There was a big door at the far end of the room. It was bolted. 'It's always bolted at night,' he explained.

He opened the door, pushed through inside. It was two big rooms knocked into one, a lounge and bedroom combined, with a curtain separating off the bedroom section. As soon as we were inside, Moira, still wearing the blood-red frock, got up quickly from the settee, ran down toward us.

Rawlins grabbed her by the arms, held her tightly. 'It's all right, Moira,' he said gently. 'I've brought a friend.'

She sure was beautiful. But it was a kinda dead beauty. There was no life in her face, no expression in her eyes. Her eyes were as black as her hair. The pupils were contracted almost to pinpoints. Her voice was low and desperate. 'I've gotta get outta here,' she panted. 'You've gotta let me go. I've gotta get out of here.'

'Tomorrow, Moira,' he soothed. 'You can go tomorrow.'

She wrenched herself away from him, viciously hacked at his shins with her high heels. It musta hurt him like hell. He grabbed her again, held her firmly but gently. 'You should go to bed now, Moira,' he said soothingly. 'Have a nice long sleep. Tomorrow you can go out for a little while, maybe.'

She became suddenly limp in his arms. 'All right, Father,' she said obediently. She turned away from him dully and, as he relaxed, spun around quickly, smashed her knuckles into his face, pushed past him blindly and tore at my cheeks with taloned fingers when I got between her and the door. I grabbed her wrists, tried to hold them. She acted like she was off her head. 'Let me go,' she screamed. 'Let me go.' And all the time she was twisting and squirming, kicking, spitting and biting, trying to get at the door, which she knew was no longer bolted.

We took an arm each, gently propelled her to the bedroom, sat her on the bed, held her until she subsided, moaning piteously and trembling like she had a fever. The hurt in Rawlins' eyes as he watched her showed the strain he was undergoing. It was a marked contrast to Moira, who behaved as though he was a complete stranger.

I leaned over, took Moira's other wrist. I looked at Rawlins meaningfully, nodded my head to him. It was a quiet instruction to beat it. As soon as he'd slipped away, she redoubled her efforts. I held her tightly. 'Don't think you're gonna get out of that door, honey,' I gritted. 'I'm stopping with you. We're gonna be here together. And I'm gonna hold you this way just as long as necessary.'

'I've gotta get outta here,' she said mechanically. 'I'll go crazy. You can't do this to me. I'll go off my head.'

'You need a nice long sleep,' I said.

She relaxed. It was what I was waiting for. I let go of her, ran back swiftly along the corridor. She had to circle the bed to follow. I got through the door, slammed it behind me before she reached it. Rawlins was waiting and ready. He slammed home the bolts. He was mopping his forehead. His face was white and drawn, his blue eyes still showing his hurt.

'You see the way it is,' he said.

'Yeah,' I said. I was thinking of him more than the dame.

'I've gotta have someone around,' he said. 'Someone to look after her.'

Matt and Tony were watching us intently. I asked, 'How long she been locked up that way?'

'About a month,' he said hopelessly. 'It doesn't get us anywhere. Somehow or other she's still getting dope. Not as much as she wants, but she's still getting some.'

I scratched my chin reflectively. 'It doesn't look such a tough proposition.'

His blue eyes lit up. 'You'll do it!' he breathed. 'I knew you'd take it on.'

'With a condition attached.' I was watching Matt and Tony. I jerked my thumb toward them. 'These two guys,' I said. 'They've gotta quit.'

'That can be easily arranged,' he said. 'They're not at all suitable. Look at the way they handled the situation this morning.'

'That's what I'm remembering,' I said grimly. I circled the table, slipped my jacket off my shoulders, tossed it into a corner. 'How about it, Matt?' I asked.

He looked at me, he looked at my fists, and he worked up a weak smile. 'Sorry about dat li'le misunderstanding dis morning.'

'So am I,' I said grimly.

He kept the table between us. When I circled one way, he circled the other. Rawlins chuckled, and Tony said: 'Give him whad for, Matt. Give him de ole one-two.'

Matt grinned weakly. 'I doan wanna cause no trouble,' he said. He looked at my angry face and fists uneasily. 'It was all a misunderstanding, and ...'

I went over the table at him, glided on my belly across the table top, clutched him around the waist so that we both hit the floor together. I hung one on his jaw, climbed to my feet and was waiting for him when he got up. He hadn't appreciated that sock on the chin. It had jarred him sufficiently to annoy him. He glowered angrily, shuffled toward me with a clumsy guard. I moved in quickly, jabbed a right and a left to his jaw and moved out again. 'First you tripped me,' I panted. 'Let's even that up.' I moved in again, smashed my knuckles in the centre of his face so that it smeared his nose, covered both of us with blood.

It hurt him badly. His eyes were watering and he kept his head lowered, his arms well up. He looked like a bear the way he shuffled around.

'Then you jumped on me,' I said grimly. I moved in quick, took a hard blow to the ribs but gave him a quick left-right-left tattoo above the heart and swung over a long left that cracked against his jaw.

I stood back to give him time to recover. 'That booting in the belly hurt,' I told him.

His face was a mask of blood through which his eyes glared apprehensively. 'Please, mister,' he pleaded.

'This is for the belly,' I growled, and drove in determinedly, took a coupla hard punches on my chest and buried my fist in his solar plexus.

He went down like a sack of coal. If it'd been a ring fight, he'd have been counted out.

Rawlins said: 'I think that's enough, Janson.'

'Not yet,' I said grimly. 'I've still got a coupla pokes on the jaw to account for.'

Matt pushed himself to a sitting position, sat staring up at me with glazed eyes.

'On your feet, rabbit,' I snarled.

'I didn't mean it, mister,' he whimpered. 'I'm sorry about it. Don't hit me again.'

I glared at him in disgust. 'All right,' I growled. 'On your feet.'

There was an appreciative twinkle in Rawlins' eyes. 'You can handle yourself, son.'

'I've been around.'

Tony helped Matt to his feet. They both stared at us sullenly. Rawlins put his hand in his pocket, pulled out his wallet and peeled off a big wad of notes. He extended it toward Tony, who grabbed greedily.

'That should settle for you two boys,' said Rawlins. 'Now you can scram, both of you.'

Matt said indignantly, 'You mean you don't want us no more?'

'That's just what I mean,' said Rawlins.

Matt said, 'You ain't got no right to ...'

I cut in gently, 'You heard what Mr Rawlins said, Matt. He doesn't want you around no more. Don't you understand him?'

Matt looked at me uneasily, sidled wordlessly toward the door. Tony followed him. Matt growled resentfully: 'Well, if that's the way you want it.'

'That's the way we want it,' I said.

They slunk out, Matt leaving a trail of blood on the waxed floor.

I sighed with relief. 'I've been aching to do that ever since this morning.'

His eyes twinkled. 'That's what I figured. That's why I brought you up here.'

'And Moira too,' I said quickly.

Once again he was serious. 'Yes,' he agreed. 'And Moira too.' He looked at me anxiously. 'You'll take it on?'

I grinned ruefully. 'It seems a crazy way of spending a holiday.' I shrugged my shoulders. 'I figure it'll work.'

'That's fine,' he said. 'That's real fine. You won't regret this, and I'll see that you get well-paid.'

'I'm not interested in the dough.'

'Just the same, you'll have to be compensated for your troubles.' He glanced around the room. 'Now, let me see. I'll have a bed brought down and put over there.'

I stared at him. I looked at the door to Moira's room and I looked at the empty corner he had indicated. 'You mean I sleep here?'

'How else can you keep an eye on Moira?'

'I guess that's right,' I said. I licked my lips nervously.

'If there's anything you need at your villa I can send for it.'

'Say, you're stampeding me into this, aren't you? I didn't figure on starting tonight.'

'What difference does it make? Tonight or tomorrow?'

I shrugged. 'Okay,' I grinned. 'Have the bed brought down.'

'That's the boy,' he chuckled. He crossed to the door, opened it up. 'I'm leaving everything in your hands, son.'

'I'll do my best,' I promised.

He hesitated a moment. 'Well, goodnight.'

'Goodnight,' I said.

He paused again. He looked toward Moira's room. 'I'm relying on you from now on,' he said. 'She's in your hands … entirely!'

I knew what he meant. He'd handed her completely into my

charge. She was a dope-crazy dame who'd give her soul for drugs. She wouldn't think twice about giving herself, if it earned her even a little dope.

'You can rely on me,' I told him.

5

I was awakened next morning by the bright burst of sunlight that entered when the curtains were drawn.

I blinked my eyes, sat up in the bed and yawned. The white-coated Nipponese steward smiled a polite good morning, gestured toward a loaded tray he'd placed on a table. 'Your breakfast, sir,' he said in faultless English.

'Fine.' I glanced around, and he anticipated me, brought my dressing-gown across and helped me on with it.

I thrust my feet into my slippers, remembered my new duties and asked, 'What about her breakfast?'

He flashed a broad smile, indicated the tray. 'Breakfast for two, sir,' he said.

'Well, get another tray, take hers into her and …' I broke off.

His almond eyes flickered slightly; his face was bland as he asked, 'Is there anything more you require? Sir?'

'I guess not,' I grunted.

He bowed from the waist, glided noiselessly from the room, closed the door behind him with just a faint click. I crossed to the door, turned the key in the lock and then hid the key under my pillow.

I looked at the tray and then looked at the door leading to Moira's room. I was remembering the way she'd been the night before. Automatically I fingered my cheek that had been torn by her fingernails. Then I squared my shoulders with a come-what-may feeling. I'd taken on this job, I'd have to see it through.

I unbolted her door, opened it. I tensed myself unnecessarily. There was no sudden flurry of movement, no hurtling body with clawed fingers reaching out to rend and tear. Just the soft rustle of movement from behind the curtain where the bed was situated.

I picked up the tray, carried it through to her room, balanced it precariously on one hand while I closed the door behind me and then walked cautiously to the far end, all set to drop the tray quickly and tangle with her.

My caution was wasted. She was in bed, her waving hair a black cloud against the white pillow, her eyes closed and the sheets pulled up tightly beneath her chin. She seemed sound asleep.

I set down the tray on an occasional table, set out the cups and saucers. I looked up quickly and caught the faint flutter of her eyelids. I looked away again, removed aluminium covers from the crisply-fried bacon and flashed her another swift glance. This time I was quicker than her. I saw her eyelids drop.

'You can quit stalling,' I growled. 'I know you're awake.'

She opened her eyes then; large, black, emotionless eyes that glared hostilely.

'Who are you?' she demanded.

'I'm the new caretaker. You and me oughta be friends.'

'Why?'

I grinned at her. 'We're gonna see a lotta each other.'

She sat up in bed, propped her weight on one elbow. She wasn't looking at me now, she was looking at the breakfast tray, scrutinising it with almost forced intensity.

'Hungry?' I asked.

'Put it on the tray. Hand it to me here,' she commanded.

I hesitated a moment. I'd agreed to take on a job. That didn't include waiting on the dame. But then … it did! It included anything that would keep her away from drugs for a few weeks.

I poured coffee, arranged the knives and forks on her tray, put the plate of bacon and tomatoes in position, lifted the tray, placed it neatly on her lap.

She had to sit higher up in bed before I could do that, punch her pillows, place them in position for her head. Red musta been her favourite colour. She wore red silk pyjamas, cut Russian tunic style, the collar and cuffs a rich black.

'I want sugar,' she commanded.

I handed her the sugar bowl. She put it on one side of the tray. She stared at it with strange intensity as she helped herself to a coupla teaspoonfuls. When I reached for the bowl, she almost snarled at me. 'Leave it. Leave it where it is.'

'Don't I get any?'

She stared at me. Her eyes narrowed. 'I'll give it to you,' she said. 'Pass your cup, I'll put in the sugar.'

She acted like sugar was in short supply, watched me with cunning eyes as she dug down into the sugar bowl, helped me to a coupla teaspoonfuls. 'That's all you get,' she said. Then she looked at the sugar bowl gloatingly.

To see a dame acting that way first thing in the morning gave me the shivers. I ate my own breakfast at the table, watched her all the time. Her appetite was small. She pecked at her food, pushed it on one side, half-finished. There was a strange, brooding, waiting attitude about her. It was as though she was waiting for me to go, as though she wanted to get me out of her way.

Her eyes worried me. Those dilated pupils made her seem inhuman. She looked such a nice kid, too.

'Sleep well last night?' I asked conversationally.

The black eyes switched to me, stared hostilely, with a glint of cunning deep down in them. 'What do you care?' she demanded.

It was then I noticed her hands. They were trembling slightly. And her face was pale, whiter than it should have been.

'Listen, Moira,' I said earnestly. 'I want you to understand. I want to help you. That's what your father wants too. I know it's tough on you, being shut up here. But it's for your own good.' I took a deep breath. 'You probably know as well as I do that when you break the habit, you're free of it for all time.'

Her eyes were still cunning. 'I don't like you,' she gritted. 'I hate you. I hate having you around.'

'That's too bad,' I drawled. 'Because you're gonna see a lotta me.'

Her knuckles were white as she gripped the tray. But even her fierce grip didn't stop her hands from trembling. She said abruptly, 'Get me my dressing-gown. It's in the wardrobe over there.' She nodded imperiously toward the cupboard.

Again I hesitated. I got up reluctantly, crossed to the wardrobe, opened it up. There was a long range of clothes hanging on the dress rail. I sorted through them, found a long blue dressing-gown.

When I carried it back to her she stared at me with a triumphant glitter in her eyes, pushed the tray toward me. 'Take this,' she ordered. 'I don't want it anymore.'

I had the uneasy feeling she was elated at having scored an advantage over me.

I took the tray, piled the used breakfast dishes on it. I was keyed up all the time, expecting any minute she would make a dash for the door. But she didn't. She kinda leaned back on the pillows, watched me through half-closed eyes with a triumphant smile tugging at the corners of her mouth.

'What are you aiming to do this morning?' I asked.

'Stop in bed,' she said. 'Bring me the papers, will you?' She raised her hand to push her hair back behind her ears; her hand was trembling like she was experiencing uncontrollable excitement.

'I'll get you the papers,' I growled.

She lay there quietly, watched me as I carried the tray away. The half-drawn curtain cut off my view of her before I reached the door. But I was tensed, my ears alert for the soft pad of bare feet as she prepared to launch herself after me.

She didn't. She lay in bed, quiet and peaceful. I opened the door, closed it behind me and shot the bolts. I put the tray on a table, stood staring at it, scratching my chin thoughtfully. Then I sighed, unlocked my door and found my way to the bathroom.

I had almost finished dressing when Rawlins knocked, came in with a cheery 'Good morning.'

I scowled. 'Not so good,' I told him.

His blue eyes were anxious. 'How was she last night?'

I scowled even more. 'We both saw her last night. She was excited, crazy to get more supplies.'

'I can't bear to see her when she's that way,' he said quietly.

I said slowly and meaningfully, 'There wasn't a peep out of her all night, and this morning she's subdued. Sullen maybe, but she isn't crazy for it anymore.'

'That's what I was afraid of,' he said hopelessly.

I stared at him. 'You know what that means?'

'Obviously,' he said quietly. 'She's getting supplies from somewhere. I've kept her locked up. I've had two men on guard over her. But somehow she keeps getting those supplies.'

'No idea how it's done?'

He shook his head hopelessly. 'Can't figure it.'

I breathed heavily. 'I'll start from scratch right now. She's slept off the sedative effects of what she got hold of yesterday. She's already got the trembles. In a coupla hours she'll be getting out of hand. From then on, I'll watch her like a hawk.'

His face was drawn. 'I'm relying on you, Janson,' he said. 'I leave everything in your hands.'

I took her the morning newspapers. She was sitting up in bed and her eyes seemed to sparkle more. She gave me an almost mocking grin as she took the papers from me.

'When do I get to have a bath?'

I scowled. 'Later,' I said. 'Plenty of time for that.'

I left her to it, bolted the door of her room and sat around reading, waiting for her craving to get the upper hand of her. Lunchtime, when the steward brought the lunch tray, Rawlins came in with him.

'How is she now?' he asked anxiously.

'I'll go take a look,' I told him.

I came back frowning. 'Quiet as a dove,' I said. 'Her hands have stopped trembling. She hasn't even dressed herself, just lying in bed with that stupid doped expression on her face.'

'Where's she getting it?' he demanded.

'I don't know,' I said grimly. 'But I'll find out.'

I took the tray in, had lunch with her. She acted almost like a normal dame. But she wasn't normal. She was hopped up. Maintained at a level of sanity by artificial stimulation. Dope gets a grip on you like drink gets a grip, only a hundred times stronger. A drunkard gets the drinking habit so easily, so gently. Then, without realising it, he's in the grip of drink, unable to escape from the craving. First he takes a drink because all his friends take a drink. Later he drinks because he likes the taste of it. The final stages are the reverse of the beginning. He then drinks not because he likes the taste of a drink, but because it's hell to be without it.

That's the way she was, dependent upon drugs, suffering hell when she couldn't get them.

'If you're gonna be around all the time,' she said bitterly, 'you'd better tell me your name.'

'Hank,' I told her. 'Hank Janson.'

'You're getting well paid for torturing me?' she sneered.

I ignored her taunt.

'You figure you've got me stretched over a barrel,' she mocked.

I didn't say anything. I got up, took the tray from her and piled on the dishes.

'Why don't you get yourself a real job?' she mocked. 'A real job. A man's job.'

I stared at her levelly. 'I've got a job right now,' I told her. 'It's a tough job, but I'm gonna finish it. I'm gonna finish it if I have to crucify you to do it.'

She tried to stare down the fierceness of my eyes, was unable to do so. Her eyes slipped away, her fingers toyed with the coverlets. 'My father wouldn't let you do anything like that,' she said confidently.

I picked up the tray, headed toward the door. I got halfway there, turned and said menacingly, 'Maybe he won't know.'

Her eyes stared back, challengingly. But she was just a little afraid of me. 'Get out,' she snarled furiously. She gestured imperiously. 'Get out of here. Get out of my sight.'

I bit my lip, carried out the tray. Then I came back to her

room, took off my jacket slowly and deliberately.

'What do you want now?' she demanded.

'The supply you've got hidden away,' I said.

Her eyes narrowed. She worked up a scornful laugh. 'You're wasting your time. I don't know what you're talking about.'

'That's what I thought,' I said.

I went to work slowly and methodically. Even in two big rooms knocked into one, there are only so many places can be used to hide something. It had to be someplace where she could get at it easily. That meant I should be able to get at it easily also.

I had all the time in the world. I lifted the pictures on the wall, upended vases, took down every book in the bookcase, dug down in the folds of deep, comfortable armchairs. She watched all the time, taunting and sneering. But there was a hint of worry in her eyes, and her taunts were weak.

At the end of an hour there was only one place I hadn't looked. I stood up, squared my shoulders. 'Okay,' I rasped. 'Now it's your turn. Hop out of bed.'

She drew herself up haughtily. 'How dare you!' But the scared look in her eyes was more pronounced.

I flexed my arms, moved in a coupla paces. 'You coming out under your own steam, or am I going to pull you out?'

She could see by my face I meant it. She tilted back her head, opened her mouth and began to scream loud enough to bring down the walls.

Rawlins had given me a free hand. I accepted the responsibility. I moved in quickly, crooked my arm around her neck, hoisted her bodily out of bed. She didn't come easily, clawed at the coverlets, kicked with her bare feet, clung to the mattress so that it was dragged from the bed with her.

I'd taken on a job and I intended to do it. I hadn't any doubt now where she'd hidden the dope. Her frantic struggles clearly showed she'd hidden it somewhere in the bed. The difficulty was keeping her quiet while I searched for it.

I solved that problem by dragging her across to the wardrobe, thrusting her desperately-resisting body in amongst the array of beautifully-tailored dresses and locking the door on her.

Amidst her muffled screams and the frantic pummelling of her fists against the panels of the wardrobe, I methodically searched the bed, ripped off the sheets and the pillows and the mattress.

It was there right enough. She'd made a tiny tear in the mattress, slid it inside. There wasn't much to it. Just a small envelope containing five tiny packets. Each packet contained enough white powder to cover one side of a dime.

I went back through to my room, put the envelope in a desk drawer. Then I came back, squared my shoulders and opened up the wardrobe.

She burst out like a cyclone, gave a whimper that was almost a howl when she saw the tumbled bedding on the floor. She dived for it, scrabbled around the mattress like a gold prospector who's sure he's struck a rich vein. She found the tear in the mattress, inserted her fingers and felt around desperately. Then she kinda froze like she'd been shocked beyond endurance.

'I told you I'd find it,' I said quietly. 'It's where you won't get hold of it now.'

She turned around slowly, and somehow she'd become a different person. Her lips writhed back from her teeth, which now seemed yellow and wolf-like. Her eyes were gleaming madly and her chest heaved like she'd just run a mile.

'Give it to me,' she said hoarsely. 'I've gotta have it.'

'You've gotta get used to being without it,' I told her.

She'd been passive before, confident and sure of herself. The sudden realisation she had no supplies to fall back on made her suddenly afraid, shrinking from the horror of what she would endure when the craving started and she had nothing to assuage it.

'Give it to me,' she demanded again. And this time her voice was loaded with loathing, menace and madness.

I saw what was coming in every line of her body, in the mad glittering eyes and in her crooked and claw-like talons.

When she sprang, I grabbed at her wrists first. Her raking nails were the things I disliked most. She writhed in my grasp, twisted her head, and sharp teeth sank into my forearm.

I tried to shake my arm free without releasing my grip on her wrists. All the time, her teeth were sinking deeper into my arm, so that in a final spasm of agony I punched her own hand against her jaw again and again until she let go.

She was possessed of maniacal, superhuman strength and endurance. As her teeth unclenched from my forearm, her up-driven knee gouged my groin. It hurt. I gasped with the agony of it and, goaded beyond endurance, spun her backwards.

She hit the floor with her shoulders, fortunately landing on the tangled bedclothes. She rolled a coupla times, climbed to her feet, sprang at me again.

I grabbed her by the shoulders and, as her tearing fingernails streaked grooves in my forearms, thrust at her so hard that she hit the tumbled bedclothes with a thump that jolted the breath outta her.

I earned a few seconds' respite to get my breath and suck my bleeding arm. Then she was coming for me again.

This was getting monotonous. I timed it so that she ran her chin into the butt of my hand. I let my arm yield toward me with the impetus of her rush. At the right moment I shot out my arm again. It wasn't a sock on the jaw. It was a shove on the jaw. Once again she hit the tangled bedclothes. This time with her shoulders. And this time it was different. Because, by the time she began to figure out where she was, I'd rolled her over, enveloped her in a coupla sheets and was beginning to roll her in a blanket.

The bedclothing effectively swathed her arms and legs. I crouched over her, held her swaddled in blankets like she was in a cocoon. She struggled madly but uselessly, snapping her head from side to side to find a target for her sharp teeth.

'Now, listen to me, fireworks,' I growled. 'I've got the dope now. It's where you won't find it. You and me are gonna have a little competition. I'm saying you're not going to get dope. You can try just any way you know. I know how it is, baby. You ain't gonna like this one little bit. But maybe, maybe later you'll feel differently.'

Her black eyes were wild. Her mouth was wide like a cavern. She was screeching fit to burst my eardrums.

'You've got plenty to occupy your mind,' I told her. 'You can make this bed, tidy this room. You'd better take notice of what I tell you, because you're gonna need things to do to keep your mind off thinking about the craving.'

I don't know if she heard me. She was screaming perpetually, like a wolf howling into the night. I released her, grabbed my jacket and strode from the room. She tossed herself around frantically, unwinding herself from those blankets. I didn't get out of the room any too soon. As I shut the door and bolted it, her weight smashed against the panels, her small fists pummelled madly and her voice, fortunately muffled, was like the high-pitched scream of a train whistle.

There was nothing I could do about that, nothing I needed to do. Sooner or later she'd realise how futile it was or would exhaust herself.

I lit a cigarette, settled back in a chair, put my feet up on another chair and relaxed. That was gonna be most of my work from now on – relaxing and waiting.

* * *

Sitting around in the lounge with the bright sunlight streaming through the windows was more wearying than I'd thought it could be. Toward the end of the afternoon I ventured in to see how Moira was taking it.

There was a pitiful change in her. In the first flush of anger when she realised I'd taken her supplies, she'd let herself go. Now the room was a shambles, chairs lying on their sides, pictures torn down and flung across the room, books pulled from the bookcase and ripped to pieces, valuable glass and china ornaments ruthlessly smashed.

But after the spasm of anger had died away, it had left her worn out, exhausted. Her drug-riddled system was basically weak. The exertions of her sudden rage made the absence of her supplies more telling.

The white oval of her face, framed by her black hair, was whiter than I'd ever thought it possible to be. The tremor of her hands was marked now. Her attitude had changed, too. Her black eyes were pleading and desperate, her hands stretched toward me beseechingly. 'I'll go crazy,' she whispered. 'You've gotta let me have some. Just a little. You've gotta let me have some.'

'I'll think about it,' I said. 'Just you get this room tidied up. Then maybe I'll think about it.'

Her eyes gleamed. 'If I clean up, will you promise to let me have some. I'll be ever so quick about it.'

'I won't promise,' I said. 'But clean up just the same.'

I left her then, spun on my heel and closed the door behind me. I bolted it firmly. I was sweating, and it wasn't the weather that was causing it. To see her white-faced, pleading and with those trembling hands, was disturbing. And this was only the beginning. This was the first stage, when she'd been without for just a few hours. It was the other and later stages that would be terrible. I could sympathise with Rawlins, understand why he couldn't bear to see her this way. I was finding it nerve-wracking myself.

Rawlins came along later. We talked for a while, played chess and finally played poker for dollar stakes. He was still with me when the Nipponese steward brought the dinner.

Rawlins had dinner with me in my room. The steward laid the table, put Moira's food on a tray. I didn't know how Moira was gonna be. I told the steward to carry the tray, opened up the door to Moira's room and led the way in.

She was slumped in a chair like she was lifeless. She sat up abruptly when she saw me, and her eyes narrowed hungrily. She stared at the tray like it was the main thing in her life. As the steward set out the meal on a table, she watched him intently, the tip of her pink tongue moistening the corner of her mouth. Her hands were trembling now like she had the ague.

I looked around the room. She'd cleaned it up, straightened

out the disorder and pushed the broken glass and china into a corner.

'Hungry?' I asked.

She didn't look at me. She pulled a chair up to the table, reached with trembling fingers for the knife and fork. The steward poured coffee and she bared her teeth at him.

'Leave me alone,' she rasped. 'Both of you. Get out of here. Let me eat in peace.'

The steward's yellowy face was expressionless. I caught his eye, motioned with my head. He followed me from the room. I bolted the door behind me, and Rawlins' blue eyes were fastened on mine enquiringly.

'The craving's there,' I said. 'It's not too strong at the moment. She's suffering a reaction. Later it'll come back stronger. That's when we'll have real trouble.'

'How long will it be before …?' his voice broke.

'Tonight maybe. Maybe the morning. I can't tell. Everything depends on her bodily strength, her resistance, and the amount of dope she's accustomed to.'

We ate our meal almost in silence. I could tell Rawlins was worried out of his life. When the steward came to collect the dishes, I went into Moira's room, collected her tray. She was lying on the bed then, docile, staring at me with black, inscrutable eyes.

'That's the idea,' I said cheerfully. 'See if you can get some sleep.'

She stared at me, didn't say anything. Her eyes watched me all the way to the door. There was something strangely unsettling about those eyes. I could feel them boring into my back almost triumphantly.

Rawlins and I played more poker, then went back to chess. Finally, he looked at his watch and said: 'It's kinda tough for you, being walled up here on your vacation.'

I shrugged. 'I'm not complaining.'

'It's late,' he said. 'But it wouldn't harm you to get out for a while. Say, two or three hours. I'll stick around until you get back.'

What he said made sense. I'd been in all day, almost like a prisoner in a cell. I needed exercise, and this was a good opportunity to get it.

'You'll keep an eye on things?'

'I'll wait here in case there's an emergency. But I promise you, nobody's going in or out of that room. Not even me.'

'I won't be more than a coupla hours,' I told him.

When I reached the door he yelled, 'Hey. Catch!'

'What is it?'

'Take my car,' he said. 'Maybe you'll need it.'

I caught his car keys, thrust them into my pocket and grinned. 'Think of everything, don't you?'

'I try to,' he said wearily. 'I try to.'

6

Not long after the lights had clicked off and the crowds had dispersed, she came out of the booth. She saw me, but there was no welcome in her eyes as I adjusted my pace to hers, walked beside her.

'I didn't see you on the beach this morning,' I said.

'I purposely kept away.'

I sighed. 'What's wrong with me? Do I smell or something?'

'There's nothing wrong with you,' she said. 'You're a nice guy. Now beat it, will you?'

'I'll walk you home.'

'I suppose I can't stop you,' she sighed. 'Aw, cut it out,' she added, swiftly countering my attempt to hold her arm.

'Why the brush-off?' I demanded. 'Why play hard to get?'

She tightened her lips, quickened her pace. I kept level with her easily. 'You're not crazy enough to figure you can outwalk me?'

'Be a good guy, will ya?' she pleaded. 'Beat it. I forgot myself the other night. There's nothing to it. You're wasting your time.'

'I'm entitled to. I'm on holiday.'

She clammed up after that, didn't speak another word all the way back to her home. I followed her up the steps into the darkened porchway, waited while she fumbled in her bag for the key. 'Do I rate a goodnight kiss?' I asked.

Her face was a white blur through the darkness. Her voice was strained. 'Why don't you cut it out? Why don't you beat it, leave me alone?'

I moved in very slowly, giving her plenty of time to react. She reacted right enough. She backed a coupla paces and her voice heightened a pitch.

'No, Hank, don't. I don't want to start anything.' She sounded almost as if she was fighting with herself.

'No goodnight kiss?' I sighed.

'I'm sorry,' she whispered.

'Okay,' I said, resignedly. 'How about feeding me a cup of coffee?'

'Oh, no, I couldn't,' she faltered. For a moment she sounded almost scared. Then a new note came into her voice, almost as though she suddenly saw the solution to a problem. 'Yeah, that's right, why not?' She seemed to be wondering at her own daring. 'Come up and have a cup of coffee.'

I didn't like it. The change in her attitude was too sudden. I had an indescribable fluttery feeling in my belly. But I'd gone too far now to back out. I wasn't sure that I wanted to anyway.

'Don't make a noise,' she whispered. 'The landlady goes to bed early.'

I followed her into a darkened passage. She closed the door behind her, switched on the hall light, and I followed her up carpeted stairs to the second floor.

'You'll have to excuse the place,' she said. 'I'm a working girl.' She led the way along a corridor, opened a door at the far end, held it for me so I could precede her.

Subconsciously I noticed the light was already on when she opened the door. But I was already well into the room by the time I realised it was occupied.

I brought up short, felt the blood rush to my face as I found myself staring into the cool grey eyes of the fella seated the other side of the table. He was pale, lean-faced, but handsome in a weak kinda way. He was so fair his hair was almost white.

The click of the door as Jane closed it behind me kinda snapped the tension. She said casually, 'John, I want you to meet a friend of mine. Mr Janson. Hank Janson.'

The cool grey eyes softened into a welcome in which the hint of suspicion lingered.

'This is John, Hank,' she said quietly. 'My husband!'

The blood musta been staining my cheeks crimson. Not for one moment had she in any way suggested she was married. Then for some crazy reason she'd brought me up here, confronted me abruptly with her husband.

I gulped, sheepishly adjusted myself to the situation. I worked up a grin, and a false heartiness made me thrust my hand across the table. 'How are you, John?' I said. 'Pleased to meetcha.'

His eyes laughed, his mouth laughed. He reached across the table without getting up and, as he realised he couldn't make it, drew back, sat back in his chair, fumbled with his hands.

I didn't get it right away. I stared. I shouldn't have done. But then, I didn't understand until his fumbling hands got the chair into movement, swivelled it around, guided it from behind the table and within reach of my extended hand.

I felt his fingers, firm and cool. But I was staring at his legs. From the waist down, his body was shrunk and wasted. I gulped, felt that shocked, fluttery feeling in my belly again.

His voice was low, musical, no trace of bitterness in it, only sympathetic understanding. 'Jane didn't tell you, then?'

I gulped, looked at Jane wildly, then looked back into his grey eyes. 'Gee, I'm sorry,' I faltered. 'I didn't know, and I musta been staring ...'

He chuckled. 'Don't worry about it. Jane should have warned you. It must have been a shock, not knowing.'

I didn't know where to look. I didn't want him to see the compassion in my eyes, didn't want to look at his wasted body and didn't want Jane either to sense the pity inside me.

'It's a funny thing,' he said casually. 'I'm the guy that's crippled. I'm the guy that should be embarrassed. But every time I meet folks, it's always them that are embarrassed.'

I forced myself to look at him. 'I asked Jane to invite me up for a coffee ...' I began.

'Sure,' he said heartily. 'It's a real fine idea. Just you sit down, make yourself at home. Jane says I'm no good at making coffee. I'd like your opinion.'

He spun one of the wheels of the chair, set off across the room toward the tiny stove. Jane was after him immediately, holding the back of the chair. 'Oh, no you don't,' she said commandingly. 'You're going to sit and entertain Mr Janson while I make the coffee.'

'But I make such good coffee ...'

'Just don't argue with me,' she said firmly. The smile on her lips denied her mock domineering, as she turned his chair around, wheeled him back toward me.

He shrugged his shoulders ruefully, sighed audibly and said, 'These women! You can never get your own way.' He gestured toward a chair. 'Sit down, old man. Make yourself at home.'

I sat down, ill at ease. Jane busied herself at the stove. I glanced around the room. It was a large room. At the far end was a half-open door through which I could see dimly the outline of a bed. The room I was in musta been the lounge, the sitting-room and the kitchen all rolled into one. Yet it was a workshop, too. Because that single swift glance showed what I would have noticed straightaway had I not been double-shocked, first by meeting her husband, secondly by learning he was a cripple.

Against one wall was a small table that served as a workbench. There was a small vice screwed on it, an array of tools and some bright, shining sheets of copper. The table was low down, low enough for a guy to work at if he was sitting in a wheelchair.

Yeah, he wasn't one of those guys that sat and moped. He kept himself busy all day, cutting, hammering, filing and shaping those copper sheets with a skill that took my breath away.

Yeah, there was plenty of evidence of his skill. His work was scattered around the room. Perfect reproductions of suits of armour in miniature. Tiny copper boats fashioned with beautiful perfection, their copper sails billowing in an unseen wind; burnished, shapely bows ploughing through an invisible sea; spars, ratlines and rigging stretched taut before the force of the gale, incredibly perfect in their detailed construction.

It took my breath away just to see the beauty of those things. They weren't toys, they weren't ornaments: they were artistic achievements. Looking at his few simple tools, I was amazed he found it possible to produce them. A crouched and snarling tiger stood alert, frightening as it tensed itself to spring. A muscular Greek god was poised on one foot, in the act of running like the wind, every muscle and sinew of his body beautifully etched. A miniature Venus equipped with arms occupied the centre of the mantleshelf, displaying exquisitely-formed limbs and breasts.

I was breathless when I looked back at him. 'They're incredible,' I said. 'I've never seen anything like them.'

The cool grey eyes smiled with pleasure. 'I'm not gonna blush shyly,' he said. 'I get a kick outta praise.' His eyes were still smiling when he said, 'It's very rare I get a chance to hear folk's opinions.'

'You musta been doing this for years,' I said.

'Two years,' he said. He saw my eyes widen, and smiled broadly. 'What d'you expect? When a guy finds he's lost the use of his legs, he's gotta find something to do.'

I gulped. 'Two years ago – when it happened?'

He fumbled in his pocket, pulled out a pack of cigarettes and offered me one. 'I don't suppose Jane told you about it,' he said. 'I was a speedway rider.' He grinned ruefully. 'Took a nasty tumble.'

'Gee, I'm sorry,' I said.

He smiled. 'I knew the risks.'

'Is there ... is there no chance ...?'

'Yeah,' he said easily, 'there's a chance.' He glanced around at Jane. She was busy setting out cups, but she was listening. 'A touch-and-go operation,' he said. 'If it works, I'm okay. If it doesn't ...' He spread his hands expressively.

It was a real tragedy. A good-looking guy like him crippled. A cute dame like Jane sticking by him, tortured by frustration.

'Gonna take the risk of the operation?'

His eyes were surprised at my question. 'What do you think, brother? Just so soon as I raise the dough, I'm going to hospital for that win-or-lose chance.'

Jane dropped a spoon. Her eyes were downcast as she bent to pick it up. He jerked his head toward her. 'Jane thinks I shouldn't take the risk.'

'It's a difficult decision to take.'

'Not for me.' His eyes flamed hungrily. 'Two years I've been in this chair. All I'm living for is a chance to get out of it.' He gestured quickly and fiercely. 'Don't get me wrong. Jane stands right beside me. She goes to work, pays the rent, keeps us alive.' He gestured toward the collection of his masterpieces. 'I sell a few pieces from time to time. The dough we get from that we put on one side.' He smiled so that his eyes twinkled. 'We call it "Operation Copper."'

Jane came across with the tray, set out cups of coffee and biscuits. 'Tell me if you need more sugar,' she said.

I picked up my cup, stirred it thoughtfully, tasted it and shook my head. Then I looked up, faced them squarely. 'Listen, John,' I said awkwardly. 'I wanna make one thing clear. I didn't know Jane was married. She's a real nice kid. I made a pass at her and got smacked down. I had to tell you that. I couldn't sit here talking to you, without telling you.'

He leaned forward, and his eyes were serious. 'You didn't have to tell me. I guessed as much. She's crazy, Hank. She's young, she's full of life. But she's tied herself to me, won't let go. I'm telling you, Hank, if you can get her to quit, take her away somewhere, you'll be doing her a favour.' He added, more quietly, 'You'll be doing me a favour, too.' His voice choked as he said it.

Jane chuckled. 'Don't take any notice of him. He's the one that's crazy. He's always talking like that.' She reached out, tousled his hair with an affectionate gesture that made tears prick at the back of my eyes.

'What's your racket?' he asked.

'Reporter,' I told him. I stirred my coffee some more, added thoughtfully, 'I'm on a kinda special assignment now. Very private.'

He took in the information with a little raise of his head, nodded understandingly like it was a hush-hush subject, never to be mentioned. 'Have you known Jane long?' he asked casually.

She giggled, wrinkled her nose. 'Me and Hank are bosom friends!'

He grinned. 'Don't tell me even a smart reporter forked out a buck.'

I flushed, grinned wryly. Then I got it. 'You made that tin chest!' I said.

He smiled proudly. 'My best piece of work,' he said. 'It musta been. It's earned a thousand times what I got paid for anything else.' Once again that rueful smile. 'The trouble is, the money was earned for somebody else.'

'It sure is a masterpiece,' I said. 'It fools folks plenty.'

He turned to Jane. 'Show it to him,' he said, with the unconceited pride of a craftsman.

She hesitated. 'Do you think I ought …?'

'Aw, don't be silly,' he chided. 'There's nothing to it.'

Her fingers loosened the draw-cord at her neck. She crossed her arms, took the bottom of the blouse, peeled it up over her head.

If it had been skin-colour it would have looked the real thing. It wasn't just the craftsmanship, it was genius! The firmly-sculptured breasts were perfect, right down to the tiniest detail. I'd seen Jane when she'd been wearing a taut, thin-as-silk bathing costume. Looking at her now, I hadn't the faintest doubt she fitted into it perfectly, like it was her own skin. She'd told me it was tailor-made. It certainly was.

With the pride of a craftsman he talked about it, pointed out the difficulties it had presented.

It was made in two halves, the back as beautifully-sculptured as the front. It was hinged at one side, from armpit to hip, with a cunning locking device, so that when closed around Jane, it locked itself automatically, dovetailing perfectly, with an undetachable joint.

'It's all very fine,' I said. 'But how d'you unlock it?'

John's eyes shone. 'It's a little invention of my own. There's only one way to open it. I'll show you. Got the key, Jane?'

'Oh, no,' she protested quickly. 'I can't take it off now!'

'Don't be silly, darling. I want to show him how the lock works.'

She got her handbag, fumbled in it, produced a long, thin piece of shaped copper. He took it from her, displayed it with loving fingers, indicated the intricately-carved ridges on it.

'The principle is simple,' he explained, 'but the manufacture is intricate. Everything has to dovetail perfectly. Hold tight, Jane,' he warned. At the same time, he carefully slid the copper strip into a tiny slot I hadn't noticed before, manoeuvred with deft fingers and, with an almost noiseless click, the ingeniously-constructed lock opened.

Jane firmly held the front against her. The back swung open on its hinge. And so perfectly formed to her body was it, it seemed like he was peeling off her skin.

'Gee, that's really something,' I said, awed.

Jane said, with a hint of annoyance in her voice, 'If you're quite finished …'

'I'd like Hank to see it properly, honey,' he said pleadingly.

She was angry without any reason that I could see. But she softened at the pleading in his voice. 'All right, John,' she said affectionately. 'I won't be a moment.'

She picked up her blouse, kept the copper front clamped securely to her and walked across to the bedroom, the back half flapping loosely on its hinge. We had only time to light a cigarette before she was back again, wearing her blouse, but with the copper mould in her hands. Automatically I eyed her searchingly. She hadn't taken time to coax herself into a brassiere, and the hard, firm shaping of her blouse didn't look any different from the copper mould she handed me.

Yeah, it was beautiful. The inside shaping of it was as perfect as the outside. I traced it with my fingers, felt the smoothness of his workmanship, the warmth of her body still lingering there and the moistness of it where she had sweated.

'How long does a thing like that take to make?'

'Three weeks,' he said.

'Three weeks!'

'Too long?' he asked anxiously.

'I should have thought six months.'

'I was working every day at it,' he said, as though excusing himself.

I grinned. 'I think you're a marvel.'

'He is, too,' said Jane. She slipped her arm around his shoulder, nestled her cheek against his head. 'Miss me today, honey?' she asked.

It sounded like my cue. I got up slowly, said, 'Well, thanks for the coffee, folks.'

'You're welcome,' he said.

'It's been nice meeting you both.'

Jane asked meaningfully, 'Understand the way it is now, Hank?'

I had the grace to drop my eyes. 'Sure,' I muttered. 'I see now.' I was remembering things, was pitying her. I was remembering the warmth of her lips, the burning eagerness inside her, which she was fighting all the time to kill.

'Look in anytime,' said John. 'Always pleased to see you.'

'Thanks,' I said. I was remembering he was needing money for his operation. I sauntered across to the workbench, picked up the exquisitely-formed figure of a naked girl poised to plunge into an imaginary pool. 'I kinda like this,' I said.

'You're welcome,' he said. 'You have it.'

'Thanks,' I said. 'That'll make an ideal paperweight for my desk.'

'Let me wrap it for you,' said Jane. She took it from me, wrapped it carefully in brown paper. I fumbled in my breast pocket, pulled out my wallet.

John said sharply, 'What's that for?'

I said sheepishly, 'I want to buy it, of course.'

'Nonsense,' he said. 'It's a present.' He was almost angry.

'But I didn't mean ...' I began.

Jane tucked the little packet into my pocket, steered me

toward the door determinedly. 'Now, don't start arguing, Hank,' she said. 'It's a present. We wouldn't dream of letting you pay. And you'll make us uncomfortable if you go on insisting.'

She'd got the door open by this time. I knew they'd never take my dough. I said, 'Well, it's real nice of you, but I never … meant …'

'Look in anytime you want, Hank,' called John, from his wheelchair.

'You see the way it is, Hank,' said Jane, seriously. Her blue eyes were looking into mine meaningfully. 'You understand the way it is now. It's … goodbye … Hank.'

I took her cool fingers in mine. 'You're a great kid, Jane,' I said. 'A great kid.'

And I meant it.

7

Rawlins was nodding in his chair when I got back. He jerked his head erect as I closed the door, blinked his blue eyes and then smiled with relief. 'Ah, so you're back,' he said unnecessarily.

I jerked my head toward Moira's room. 'How is she?'

'Very quiet,' he said. 'Haven't heard a sound out of her.'

'Think I'll go take a look.' I hesitated, looked at him meaningfully. 'It's been a long day. She might be difficult. You sure you want to hang around?'

His face was haggard again, his eyes worried. He licked his lips. 'I'll wait in here,' he said. 'You go right ahead.'

I unbolted the door, went through into her room. I was ready for almost anything. I couldn't believe it when I saw by the softened lights that she was sleeping peacefully. I tiptoed right up to the end of the bed, stood watching her with anger burning inside me. She smiled in her sleep, her lips parted and her breasts rising and falling softly and rhythmically.

I tiptoed out, closed the door behind me. He saw the frown on my face, asked anxiously, 'She's all right? There's nothing happened?''

'Something's happened, all right,' I said bitterly. 'Somehow, someway, she's got hold of more of it.'

His face dropped. 'It's always happening,' he said hopelessly. 'They know she's got plenty of money of her own. They get it to her somehow, someway.'

I narrowed my eyes. 'They won't do it for long,' I promised. 'I'll stop them.'

* * *

I got my first chance the next morning. I'd been doing a lot of thinking. When the Nipponese steward brought the breakfast tray, I was waiting for him. Without a word, I inspected the dishes, turned over the pieces of bacon, dug down into the sugar bowl with a spoon.

I found it in the sugar bowl. It was right at the bottom, a little package wrapped in cellophane. I spun swiftly, grabbed the steward by the throat and bent him over backwards until his spine threatened to snap. 'You swine,' I gritted. 'You ought to be cut to pieces for pulling a stunt like that.' I thrust him from me angrily, so that he sprawled backwards, hit the ground with his shoulders. He pushed himself to a sitting position. His expressionless eyes were wide in his emotionless, yellowy face. 'You are making a mistake, sir,' he said in his faultless English. 'I am affronted by the indignity brought upon me by ...'

His flat, metallic voice goaded me to madness. I rushed at him, grabbed him by the collar, half-dragged him to his feet and gave him the back of my hand full in the teeth so that he hit the floor a couple of yards away.

He sat up, spat blood and wiped his split lips. His almond eyes were narrowed slits. 'The affront afforded by this unwarranted attack ...' he began.

I was halfway toward him when the door opened. I hardly knew or cared. But Rawlins' firm, authoritative voice was like a whiplash. 'Janson!' he commanded, and there was a quality in his voice that brought me to a standstill.

He stood framed in the doorway, his blue eyes flicking from my red and angry face to the steward, who was clambering to his feet, blood trickling down his chin onto his white coat.

Rawlins breathed hard, closed the door firmly behind him. 'Now, what's going on?' he demanded.

'He's the fellow responsible,' I said bitterly. 'He's been

taking drugs in to her, right under our noses.'

His blue eyes flicked from me to the steward. 'What have you to say about this, Lin?' he demanded.

Lin dabbed at his bleeding lip. You couldn't tell from his expression whether he was pleased or happy, angry, annoyed or hurt by what had happened. In flat, even tones he said, 'Mr Janson discovered a package secreted in the sugar bowl.'

'What d'you know about it?' asked Rawlins.

'I know nothing about it, sir. The sugar bowl is kept in the pantry overnight. Almost anyone has access to it.'

'You lying little runt …' I began, making a savage movement toward him.

'Hold it, Janson,' rapped Rawlins.

'You're not gonna let that little sawn-off runt lie his head off …' I burst out.

Rawlins said quietly and softly, 'Lin has been with me thirty-five years. Throughout the whole of that time, I haven't once known him to tell a lie.'

I breathed hard, wondering how a smart guy like Rawlins could be taken in so easily. Then I gasped. 'Wait a minute,' I said. 'This goon ain't no more than twenty-five. How come you say he's been with you thirty-five years?'

The suspicion of a smile twitched at Rawlins' mouth. 'Appearances are sometimes deceptive,' he said. 'Lin is probably older than you think.' He turned to him. 'Just exactly how old are you?'

Lin made a final dab at his lips, tucked away the blood-stained handkerchief. 'I was fifty-four last June, sir,' he said.

'Fifty-four!' I echoed.

'And of one thing I'm quite convinced,' said Rawlins. 'Lin had nothing to do with this whatsoever. Somebody else planted the stuff in the sugar bowl.'

My head was going around. I stared at Lin. He looked a young man, but he was fifty-four. I'd picked him up, slammed him around like he was a young guy who could take it. I cleared my throat a couple of times, finally got the words out. 'I'm sorry, Lin. I wasn't thinking. I jumped to a natural conclusion, and …'

His face was all smiles. It was the first time I'd seen him smile. 'The injury is nothing. The affront and destruction of my dignity were a different matter. But your realisation that a mistake has been made has remedied everything.'

It was quite a speech. Most guys who'd been bounced the way I'd bounced him would have wanted to poke me on the nose. I stepped forward, offered him my hand. 'I'll make it up to you some way, Lin,' I promised.

'It is as nothing compared with the sands of time that engulf civilisation in but a small fragment of existence.'

I gulped. He'd probably studied Confucius. I hadn't. His comments went right over my head, and I let them. 'Just so long as you know I'm sorry,' I said.

'That is quite all right, sir.' His beaming face smoothed itself into its customary stone-wall expression. 'Is there anything more you will be needing, sir?'

'That's the lot, Lin,' I said. 'Much obliged.'

As he closed the door, Rawlins said. 'I'll have a man watch the kitchen. I'll find out who's planting it.'

'Are you sure of Lin?'

'Absolutely,' he said with conviction.

I scowled. 'I'll check all food from now on. If this continues, we'll never get her better.' I scowled even more. 'Think how tough it will be if she's almost at the final stage and somehow she gets hold of new supplies.'

'That's the way it is,' he said. 'She's got dough and they know it.' He looked real worried now. 'They'll get supplies through to her any way they know how, just to keep her an addict and a customer.'

I sighed. 'Well, here we go again. We'll make a fresh start now, because we're no further forward than we were yesterday.'

'I wish it were all over,' he said wearily.

I nodded toward the breakfast tray. 'I'll go see her now.'

'Anything I can do?'

'No,' I said. 'I'll handle this.' Then I hesitated. 'Yeah, there is one thing. If we can't beat this thing one way, we'll do it another. Figure out some quiet place we could take her where we'll be more isolated.'

A strange look came into his eyes. 'I've got ideas about that too,' he said. 'I've been turning it over in my mind for quite a time. But it's a tough proposition.'

'It's a tough proposition right now,' I told him.

He smiled faintly. 'I'll go into it some more. Let you know about it.'

Moira pretended to be asleep when I took in the breakfast tray. I spread out the teacups with a loud clatter, rasped in a harsh voice. 'Why do you pull that stunt? I know you're not asleep.'

She sat up in bed, pushed herself up on one elbow and smiled at me mockingly. 'How long are you gonna stick around?' she demanded. 'You give me a pain.'

I was watching her all the time. She couldn't help it. Her eyes kept flicking toward the sugar bowl. I stood so she could see me, performed the action slowly and deliberately, picked up an empty cup, picked up the sugar bowl and slowly poured the sugar into the cup.

She gave a little gasp, watched the steady stream of sugar with wide, anxious eyes that registered desperate alarm when she realised there was gonna be no drugs forthcoming that morning. Then, instinctively, her eyes flicked to the bookcase.

I'd been waiting for just such a lead as that. I was at the bookcase almost before she realised it, tearing out the books, tumbling them on the floor. As they hit the floor they spilled open. From between the pages of one of them a familiar flat packet protruded. She was way behind me, barely out of bed by the time I'd stooped, picked up the flat packet and thrust it in my pocket.

I stood grimly waiting for her, hands tensed at my sides. She musta taken a pretty large jolt of dope the night before, or even that morning. Sufficient, at any rate, to make her almost normal for the time being. She brought up short, glared at me angrily as she sensed the futility of attack.

It was in that moment that for the first time I saw her as a woman. She was wearing those blood-red silk pyjamas, and her black hair was a vivid, black velvet contrast. Her eyes sparkled angrily, the red tints in them blending with the savage redness of her apparel. She drew herself up to her full height, vibrant, tense and burning. Her burning anger accentuated her womanhood. Her youthful, vigorous body strained through the thin clothing.

I became acutely conscious we were alone together in her bedroom, that we were gonna be alone together a whole lot of the time. She was a woman, and I'd only just realised it. And from now on it was gonna be twice as difficult for me.

Her eyes narrowed. 'What d'you want for it?' she asked quickly.

'Forget it, baby,' I smiled. 'You're not getting this.'

Her eyes narrowed even more. She worked an artful, wheedling note into her voice. 'You want money? I've got plenty of money. As much as you want. We can be friends. You can get it for me every day.'

'Your breakfast,' I said shortly. 'Eat your breakfast.'

She came a coupla paces closer to me. She was breathing eagerly and excitely now. I noticed it, the way her breasts rose and fell. I wiped my forearm across my forehead. It came away damp. 'You and me can be friends,' she insisted. 'You can have all the money you want.'

I beat a rapid retreat, bolted her in the room while I locked this latest haul away with the other packets. As long as I hadn't the package on me, she'd have no incentive to attack me.

When I got back, she was sitting on the bed, scowling sullenly. 'You haven't got it with you?' she asked.

'I've scattered it,' I told her. 'You'll never see that again.'

She gave a gasp, like knowing what had happened to it gave her a pain deep inside.

'Eat your breakfast,' I said gruffly. I poured the coffee, set the table, pulled up a chair for her.

She kinda shrank into herself, hardly noticed she was eating, and was apparently oblivious of my presence. It was as though she'd sealed herself off from everything, as though her mind was concentrating intently on one single, urgent problem.

She may not have been conscious of me, but I was conscious of her. I couldn't help it. She was sitting close enough to me to touch. She was breathing, and all her body seemed to breathe. Her dainty feet were bare, and the soft silk of her pyjama trousers was strained taut across her knees and thighs so that I thought I could see the shimmer of her flesh beneath. The rounded thrust of her breasts against the tunic was uncontrolled.

The firm, clean-cut charm of Jane had been tormenting me. Jane had promoted me to record temperatures on a coupla occasions, only to dampen me down immediately afterwards. But I hadn't cooled down all that much. And right now, sitting next to Moira in the intimacy of her bedroom, and close enough to ... well, close enough, at any rate ... reminded me I was very, very human. It reminded me this job wasn't gonna be twice as tough as I'd thought, it was gonna be four times as tough.

I got up abruptly, began to pile the breakfast dishes on the tray. She said emotionlessly, like I was a servant, 'I want to take a shower.'

'I'll see about it.'

'I want to take a shower,' she repeated firmly, like she was issuing orders.

'Okay, I'll fix it,' I told her. I figured she had to wash sometimes. It was a reasonable enough request.

I bolted her in while I went along to the bathroom, inspected it. The windows were leaded, securely fastened. Only the fanlights opened, and they were too small for her to climb through, even if she'd been able to reach them.

I didn't take any chances. I inspected everything thoroughly, cleaned out the medicine chest, groped around in the ventilator, even thrust my finger up the bathroom tap to make sure nothing was secreted there.

Rawlins had said he would take Lin's word for anything. I accepted his judgment, assigned Lin to clean up Moira's room while she took her shower. Then I escorted her to the bathroom.

She carried a bathrobe with her, still wore her pyjamas. Lin supplied me with two clean towels. Moira was ready to try everything. Halfway along the corridor, she spun around, made a frantic dash for the front door.

It was all so obvious I was almost uninterested. I caught her in three strides, wrapped my arm around her waist and lugged her toward the bathroom.

She didn't resist. I guess she musta realised it was useless. But I still had my arm around her. I was actually touching her now, feeling the warmth of her skin through that silky covering.

I opened the door of the bathroom, thrust her inside. I was almost angry. I had a right to be. She was getting under my skin more and more every minute. It was getting so I couldn't take my eyes off her. And all the time my temperature was mounting I knew it wasn't gonna get me anywhere. Rawlins had placed his trust in me. I couldn't go back on him.

'Take your time,' I told her. 'Only don't get any wrong ideas. I'm gonna be right outside this door until you're through. And what's more, you can't lock the door. I'm warning you, if you try anything, I'll be coming in after you.'

She tossed her head, slammed the door. I sighed, pushed the chair I'd placed ready across the doorway, sat down, lit a cigarette.

She sure took her time. I listened to the hiss of the shower, listened to the water from the bath tap. She musta soaked in four or five different lots of water. Finally she was through, opened up and almost stumbled over me as I straddled the doorway.

There were a lotta changes in her now. Her eyes had lost a lotta their life. Her face was white and her hands were trembling. The last lotta dope was wearing off.

There were other changes too. She was carrying her pyjamas over her arm, was wearing only the bathrobe. It was a skimpy bathrobe, finished a long way short of her knees, was loosely tied so that it showed a sharp white vee at her neck.

We-walked back along the corridor side by side. I was scared. I was scared she'd try and make a break for it again. If she did, I'd have to grapple with her. It made me breathless to think of grappling with her, dressed the way she was.

But she didn't make a break for it. She walked back to her room like she was in a dream. I opened the door for her, and as she entered, Lin came out. I closed the door behind her, bolted it firmly.

'Anybody been in that room except you?' I rasped.

'No, sir,' he said in his flat tones. 'I have cleaned the room and there has been nobody in there except me.'

'That's fine,' I grunted. 'Now we see what lunchtime brings.'

* * *

Lunchtime was good, and yet it was bad. By then she was prowling the room like an angry tigress. She'd been throwing things all over the room, and as soon as I entered, she sprang at me with a wild look in her eyes, white teeth flashing and nails upraised to rend and tear.

I ducked back quickly, got the door closed while I issued fresh instructions to Lin. In Moira's present mood it would be crazy to give her knives and forks and crockery. He came back with food minced on an enamel plate and ready to be eaten with a spoon.

I waited until she was quiet, slipped inside her room, put the food on the floor, slipped out again before she could reach me.

I breathed a sigh of relief when I bolted the door.

Rawlins came in later.

'She's on the run,' I told him. 'She's out of supplies, nerves worn ragged by it. She'll probably get worse.'

'Look after her, Hank,' he pleaded. 'She's all I've got. I don't want anything to happen to her.'

'I'll watch her,' I promised.

We played chess for a coupla hours and then it started. Her voice was piteous and beseeching on the other side of the door. Then it became frantic, coupled with the urgent pummelling of her knuckles against the door panels. She kept it up until she sank to the floor exhausted. Then a little later it started all over again, a piteous, inhuman pleading that drove me crazy.

Rawlins couldn't stand it. Shortly after it began, he got up, white-faced, excused himself quickly and went out. I couldn't do that. I had to sit there and take it, listen to her wild pleading and sobbing until I thought I'd go crazy myself.

It lasted three or four hours. Then it stopped abruptly. I tiptoed to the door, listened, heard her dragging footsteps.

After that there was silence. I wanted to go into her, yet daren't. It sounded like she had quietened down from exhaustion. If only I could get her to drink a sedative now, by the morning she would have been a full twenty-four hours without drugs. One whole day without drugs! That would leave just thirteen more days to complete the cure. Thirteen more days, I reflected bitterly, and shuddered. Just one day had been hell.

My own nerves were worn ragged by the time Lin arrived with the dinner tray. I motioned to him to put it on the table. 'I'll go see how she is,' I told him. 'I shouldn't wonder if she's in no mood to eat tonight.'

I unbolted her door, entered cautiously. I could see her right away. She was slumped in an armchair at the far end, wearing that blood-red dress she'd been wearing when I first saw her. I walked toward her slowly, cautiously. Her black eyes were watching me. She seemed exhausted. Her face was white and she was suffering acutely. I could tell that by the way her lips kept twitching and her hands trembling.

I went right up to her, stood over her, staring down at her. 'How d'you feel?' I asked.

She opened her lips, said in a weak voice, 'I'm ill. I think I'm dying. I've got a pain here.' As she spoke, she sat up, her face contorted in agony, and both hands went to her belly. I bent over her and, as I did so, she kinda flopped back in the chair, limbs rigid and eyes staring. Her mouth moved strangely, like she was chewing her lips, and red froth bubbled from her mouth. Her eyes were staring, horrible and frightening. She gave deep, low-shuddering gasps, and all the time her body jerked like she was suffering excruciating agony.

I wasn't a doctor but I knew dope wouldn't cause this. There was something very wrong with her. Maybe she'd taken poison. Yeah, that was it. She'd got hold of poison somehow, had taken it. A frenzied urgency dominated my mind. I thought of a hospital wagon, clean white beds and a stomach pump, as her body jerked in agony, her eyes started from her head and the red froth bubbled over her chin.

I ran swiftly back to my room, grabbed Lin by the shoulder, thrust him toward the corridor. 'Get Mr Rawlins right away,' I ordered. 'It's urgent.'

Unblinkingly he accepted my order, slipped away like greased-lightning. I ran in the opposite direction down the corridor toward the study. I grabbed the phone, dialled emergency.

The doctor was still taking down the address when Rawlins burst into the study with Lin right behind him. 'Where is she?' he panted.

'Don't know what it is,' I told him. 'She looks pretty bad to me ...' I broke off.

He stared back at me. 'She's not in her room,' he said.

I drew a deep breath. I said into the telephone, 'I'm sorry, doctor. It was a false alarm. Please don't bother to come now.'

I hung up slowly. Rawlins' shoulders drooped. 'I'll have them search the house,' he said hopelessly. 'I don't suppose it'll be any use.'

My own shoulders drooped. 'She looked like she was dying,' I excused myself. 'I thought she'd taken poison somehow.'

'Forget about that now,' he snapped. 'The main thing is to get her back here as soon as possible. Well, what is it?' he snapped irritably as the butler appeared in the doorway.

'Excuse me, sir,' said the butler. 'The gardener has just reported to the kitchen. He said that a few minutes ago Miss Moira cast off the launch and headed in the direction of town.'

Rawlins took it quietly. 'Very well, Meakins,' he said.

I strode grimly toward the door.

'Where are you going, Janson?' he asked.

'I'm gonna get her,' I gritted. 'I'll bring her back.'

'I'm sorry about it, Janson,' he said quietly. 'I should have warned you.'

I was remembering the way she'd insisted on having a shower. I was remembering the red foam on her lips, remembering that the soap in the bathroom had been red. Dope made that dame as sharp as knives. My bet was she'd have convinced even a doctor she was dying.

'She's done this before,' he said, unhappily. 'She'll run the launch up on the beach near town. She usually takes an overdose. The police find her wandering in the streets later, book her as a drunk.'

'I'll go get her,' I said quietly.

'It'll be difficult to find her,' he said. 'You can take your time. You can't get to town before her. By sea it's direct, by road it's a long way round.'

'I'll get her,' I said.

'And when you get back,' he said, 'we'll have to talk. I've been working on a proposition I want to put to you.'

I breathed hard. 'I'm in up to the neck,' I told him. 'I'm gonna see this through now, right to the end!'

8

I found where she'd driven the launch up onto the beach some three hundred yards away from the fairground. Moira musta cast off from the landing stage, notched the engine to full speed and used the lights of the fairground as a target. It was a high-powered launch, built for speed, and had cost plenty. Luckily the sand was soft, otherwise she'd have ripped the bottom out of it. As it was, she'd driven half its length up onto the sand.

At first thought, it seems crazy for a guy to go looking in a big town for a drug-crazy dame and expect to find her. But I didn't figure it was gonna be all that difficult. I'm a reporter, and any reporter worth his salt gets around, gets hunches that work out, knows instinctively what kinda district he wants and knows it when he gets there.

Long View Beach was a busy town. It was a free town, too. You could gamble openly, and gambling saloons invited custom with bright neon lights.

Wherever you get gambling you get what goes with it. One good racket is never enough. A good racketeer is always wanting to spread his wings. Vice is his business, and he operates vice every way he knows how. The successful racketeers dovetail the vice rackets so that the suckers are led quite naturally from one to the other. I played the part of the tourist, lost a few bucks on the gambling tables, drank a little and walked like I'd drunk a lot. When a seedy little guy sidled alongside me and whispered from the corner of his mouth, I nodded vaguely, stumbled after him into the backstreets, along dimly-lighted cobbled alleys.

There was plenty of variety to choose from, a coupla narrow streets specialising in the particular entertainment the seedy-looking guy had suggested. We walked along narrow pavements lined with brightly-lighted windows. Dames leaned on the sills of the open windows, smiled temptingly and named their price.

We toured the streets three times and I still wasn't getting onto anything. The seedy little guy became aggressive. 'Look, mister,' he growled. 'You wanna good time, so I show you. Then you say it ain't what you want. What the hell are you after? Just give me a buck and I'll call it a deal, leave you to it.'

I gazed at him blearily. 'The dames are okay,' I slurred. 'But I wanna little excitement, pal. Something that'll give a guy a real thrill.'

He eyed me narrowly. 'Just what do you want?' he demanded bluntly.

I stared at him owlishly. Then I made the pantomime of putting a cigarette to my mouth, lighting it slowly, breathing it in deeply and then sighing with pleasure. Only I wasn't thinking of a cigarette. I was thinking of a reefer. And he knew it.

He was a tout, the worst kind. A mean guy who got his living from commission on the sale of women's bodies. But deep down inside him there musta been a spark of decency. 'Look, fella,' he warned. 'You ever had that stuff? Because if you haven't, lay off.'

I bleared, swayed lightly, rested one hand on his shoulder. 'I'm hungry for it, pal,' I slurred. 'I ain't had a sniff since yesterday. I'm getting kinda burned up on account of it.'

He stared at me solemnly. Then he shrugged my hand off his shoulder. 'You can find your own way, fella,' he grunted. 'You can try Joe's. You can't miss it. Third left and first right.'

'Who do I ask for?' I blurred.

'You're on your own,' he said. 'I don't handle this thing.' A crafty look came into his eyes. 'How about a buck, mister? I've spent a lotta valuable time on you.'

I gave him five bucks. I meant to. It served my purpose, because he thought I'd made a mistake, disappeared swiftly before I should find out.

Still swaying and singing softly to myself, like a guy who's taken enough on board to be happy, I steered my way past the lighted windows and inviting voices toward Joe's.

Joe's was the kinda joint I was looking for. I knew it in my bones. The district itself was sufficient: dimly-lighted windows with firmly closed doors, black alleyways leading off into impenetrable darkness, grey figures lurking at corners, and the occasional red eye of a cigarette from a darkened doorstep.

Joe's was a low-down bar. I pushed through swing doors into a thick, smoky atmosphere that I smelled right away was tainted with marijuana. The vice-kings musta got the cops on their payroll. Things weren't exactly run in the open, but a cop would have had to have had only half an eye to know there was a back room to that joint, and what went on in it.

There were three or four guys sitting at tables, a group of young folk at the far end, numbering among them two fluffy-haired dames who were giggling most of the time.

I eased across to the counter, leaned my elbows on it and stared at the bartender thoughtfully. He stared back, sharp-eyed, fleshy-faced and sweating visibly.

'What's on your mind?' he demanded.

'Can I get a little service?'

'Sure. What d'you want?' he asked. 'Scotch? Beer?'

'A smoke,' I leered.

He stared at me. He stared at me so long I thought he'd lost his voice. Finally he said, 'It costs plenty.'

'I've got plenty,' I boasted. 'I just wanna little excitement.'

He jerked his head to the door at the far end of the bar. 'Through there,' he said curtly.

I swayed a coupla times walking toward the door. There was a sallow-faced guy sitting beside it. He intercepted a glance from the bartender, nodded understandingly and let me pass through.

It was like walking into a Chinese temple that's been burning joss-sticks for a coupla months. It was a long, narrow room, brick-lined and looking more like a long cellar than anything else. Bunks lined the walls either side, with drawn curtains like a sleeping car. Some of the curtains were open, showing guys reclining on cushions, drawing steadily on reefers or tossing around in some nightmare delirium.

What was happening on the bunks where the curtains were drawn wasn't difficult to imagine. I'd hardly got into the room before I was surrounded by a group of dames. One of them grabbed my left arm and smiled into my face. The others melted away discreetly. 'You wanna smoke, honey?' she drawled.

'Sure, that's the idea.'

Already she was leading me along the aisle between the bunks. She was dark, with straight hair cut short with a fringe across the forehead. It gave her a Chinese appearance, which was added to by the long, thin line she'd made of her eyebrows and the narrowness of eyes. There was no doubting she was a woman. She wore a loose white silk tunic that reached to just below her waist, and nothing more.

'You'll be comfortable here, honey,' she drawled, and steered me into an unoccupied bunk.

I rolled onto it, propped my shoulders against the pillows. She bent over me, fluttered her eyelids half-a-dozen times and patted my cheek. 'You wanna reefer, honey?' she invited.

'Sure,' I said.

'Ten bucks,' she said, and held out her hand.

I gave a whistle of indignation.

She smiled coyly, dropped her eyes. 'That's with me, too, honey.'

I grinned. 'That's different.' I fumbled in my pocket for a ten-spot. Her eyes watched attentively. I was too smart to flash my roll. I already had loose dollars in my trouser pockets.

She was quick at taking the dough. She had it out of my hand as soon as I produced it. 'I won't keep you a moment, honey,' she said, and slipped away.

She was back quickly. She nudged me to move over, climbed

in, knelt on the bunk beside me while she pulled the curtains.

The curtains were thin. The light that seeped through them gave all that was needed.

She put a reefer between my lips, put one in her own mouth. Then she looked at me expectantly. With her get-up, she couldn't have carried around a postage-stamp. She certainly wasn't carrying a box of matches. I reached up, pulled the reefer from between her lips. She stared at me with astonished eyes. I put my hand behind her neck, pulled her down toward me. She understood then. She came smoothly, easily.

I pulled her across the other side of me, jammed her between myself and the wall. Her soft fingers caressed my cheek and she said huskily, 'Gee, honey! You're cute!'

I slipped my fingers around her neck and she gave a little shudder of pleasure. I probed gently for the right spot, found it, and suddenly turned on the pressure. Her mouth opened and her eyes were wide and staring. But the scream was stifled in her throat, and my fingers were like steel bands, threatening to plunge her into eternal darkness.

'I'm gonna give you a chance,' I whispered quickly. 'I'm gonna ease off. But if you start to scream, by heaven I'll choke you. I mean it.'

She was rigid in my arms. I could feel her heart beating madly.

'You understand me?' I gritted. 'If you do, nod your head.'

I felt her trying to nod her head. I took a deep breath, gently eased the pressure on her neck. She knew and I knew that in the fraction of a second I could tighten the pressure of my two thumbs, gouge them deep into her wind-pipe, strangle a scream before it was born and throttle her silently without anyone being any the wiser.

'You're a smart kid,' I whispered. 'Right now you're in a jam. But if you go on being smart, you can get out of it easy and make plenty of dough for yourself too.'

Her eyes strained painfully to look into my face. Her lips worked to form words I couldn't understand. I released the pressure on her neck a little more and she panted: 'What d'you want? What are you after?'

'A little information,' I said. 'It's between you and me. Nobody else need know. And it earns you a hundred bucks.'

Her eyes gleamed when she heard the sum of money I mentioned. Then they narrowed, became loaded with suspicion. 'This is a tough outfit, fella,' she whispered. 'I'm not risking my neck. What is it you wanna know?'

'The Rawlins girl,' I said. 'I wanna know where she is.'

Up until this moment she'd been tensed. Now she relaxed. It was as though she was getting a respite from a terrifying strain. She even chuckled huskily.

'What's so funny?' I demanded.

'It's a relief,' she smiled. 'I thought you were wanting real information.'

'It's real as far as I'm concerned. I'm willing to pay for it. A hundred bucks.'

Again there was that hungry glint in her eyes at the mention of money. 'All right, fella,' she said. 'You can cut out the rough stuff. I'm not squawking.'

I eyed her calculatingly. I judged she was too interested in dough to raise a squawk. I took a chance and released her.

She propped herself up on her elbow alongside me. Most of her was overlapping on to me. It was hot in that cubicle, the atmosphere thick with the scent of marijuana. I fancied I could smell her, too, feel the heat of her against me.

'The Rawlins girl is not here,' she said.

'She's in town,' I told her. 'She came tonight. She's here somewhere. I wanna know just where.'

She eyed me thoughtfully. 'You're one of the guys hired to get her off dope?' she guessed.

'What's it to you? You'll get paid.'

Her eyes were wide and thoughtful. She watched my face, weighed her advantage with the care of a bank clerk paying out dough. 'Two hundred bucks,' she said, finally.

'It's a deal if I find her.'

'You'll find her,' she said confidently.

'Okay. How do I start?'

'You'll have to wait for me. I'm off in a coupla hours. My early night.'

'Okay. Where do I wait?'

She grinned at me. 'Why not wait here?'

'I prefer the fresh air,' I growled.

Her hand was detaining on my shoulder as I half rose. 'I'm through in a coupla hours,' she said. 'But that's provided I haven't got a customer. You be my customer. I'm sure of getting off then.'

'That's a deal too,' I grunted. 'But it's business; strictly business.'

'That's okay by me,' she said coolly. 'D'you think I wanna slave myself to death?'

She rolled away from me, propped herself up against the cushions on the other end of the bunk so that she was facing me. She stretched her legs out in front of her, long supple limbs that were smooth and white. 'When do I get the dough?' she asked.

'You're sure you can find out where she is?'

'Don't you worry about that,' she said confidently.

'I'll give you half now and a half when I find her.' I fumbled in my hip pocket.

'Be your age,' she said. 'Keep your dough in your pocket.'

I stared at her.

'I told you this is a tough outfit,' she said. 'You pay me the dough outside. Pay me now and I'll never get it outside.' Her hand indicated the short tunic explanatively. 'This thing's got no pockets, and we're searched thoroughly for concealed dough before we get our outdoor clothes. They'd even notice if you went out with one tooth more than you came in with.'

I looked at her thoughtfully. She was pretty, in a vulgar kinda way. 'How long you been working here, kid?'

Her face hardened, her eyes glittered. 'What's it to you?' she sneered.

I shrugged. 'Skip it. Just trying to make conversation.' I fumbled in my pocket, produced a pack of cigarettes, offered her one and lit up.

She nestled her shoulders more comfortably against the

cushions, leaned back her head to blow smoke through her nostrils and moved her legs. It was hot in that cubicle. I was sweating. And while she seemed completely unconscious of the brevity of her tunic, I was acutely conscious of it. It seemed the gods were conspiring to provide me with an ever-mounting temperature while withholding my right to do anything about it.

Yeah, I sure was sweating in that cubicle. But a guy who's been around as long as I have and seen the things I've seen doesn't tangle with a dame in a dump like that, no matter how attractive she appears.

The dame took it quietly, sat there with bare legs brazenly displayed, smoking my cigarettes one after the other. As for me, I thought I'd never get through those two hours.

But time always passes, no matter how slowly. 'Okay,' she said at last. 'There's ten minutes to go. You beat it now. Wait for me outside.'

It was a relief to get out in the open, breathe pure air that wasn't tainted with the cloying smell of marijuana. I paced up and down, waiting for her, and got my temperature halfway down toward normal.

She came out from a side door, clip-clopped toward me on high-heels, her steps stunted by the tight skirt she wore, and with a tall feather protruding jauntily from an absurd little hat.

She didn't look the same girl with clothes on. I stared at her, having difficulty recognising her without her make-up. She took my arm confidently, steered me along the sidewalk, her high-heels clip-clopping three times to my one. 'Have you got the dough, honey?' was her first question.

I had the hundred bucks ready. I gave it to her. She glanced at it swiftly, checked the amount and then thrust it quickly into her bodice, like she was afraid someone might see her. 'It's not far,' she said. 'And I get the other hundred bucks when you find her?'

'That's the idea.'

She steered me around another coupla streets, stopped at a bar, jerked open the door and called inside. 'Anyone seen Pokey around?'

The fifth bar we called at she got a lead. We followed it, found Pokey in a bar just twenty yards from where we'd started at Joe's.

He was a sallow little guy, ferrety-eyed and flashily dressed. He stared at the dame piercingly when she entered, and then his eyes switched to me, suffused with a hungry glint.

She crossed to him quickly, dragging me with her. 'Hello, Pokey,' she said breathlessly. 'Have a good night?' There was a kinda eager sparkle in her eyes, as though she wanted to be especially nice to him.

He looked at her steadily. 'Who's the guy?' he rasped.

'He's all right. He's a gentleman friend.'

The ferrety eyes examined me calculatingly.

'I just earned a hundred bucks,' she said breathlessly. She glanced around swiftly to make sure we weren't being overheard, dived her hand into her bodice, pulled out the little wad of bills.

His action was automatic. He reached out, took the bills, tucked them in his pocket. There was an almost childish look of dismay on her face. He saw it, said roughly, 'Don't worry, I'll give you some dough later.'

I cleared my throat. 'Look,' I said grimly. 'She ain't earned that dough, yet.'

His eyes narrowed. 'Don't get impatient, fella. She's gotta key. She'll give you a good time.'

I could happily have pounded my knuckles again and again into his twisted little mouth. I could cheerfully have taken him by his large ears, battered his head against the counter. But it wouldn't have got me what I wanted. And it wouldn't have made any difference. The dame was devoted to him, she worshipped him, gladly gave him her earnings so that he could lounge around in bars, wearing flashy suits.

She interrupted quickly. 'It's something else he wants, Pokey.' She glanced around again, lowered her voice conspiratorially. 'The Rawlins dame's in town. He wants to find her.'

The ferrety eyes brightened, examined me more closely. 'How bad d'you want to find her?' he demanded.

'There's another hundred bucks coming when he does find her,' she said breathlessly.

'Another hundred bucks,' he repeated thoughtfully.

She turned to me. 'Pokey knows where she is. He knows everything. He goes around every night checking up on supplies.' She broke off abruptly, bit her lips as she intercepted a murderous glare from Pokey.

I said quickly, 'I just wanna know where she is. Beyond that, neither of you are involved.'

He said slowly, 'It'll be a hundred and fifty bucks.' His eyes were hard and calculating. I could tell from the way he held his breath he was afraid he was driving too hard a bargain. But dough didn't worry me. It was the dame I was after.

'It's a deal,' I said.

Pokey called the bartender, paid his bill. Without a word, he walked out. The dame clip-clopped after him, hung on to his arm possessively. He was an unpleasant little runt and she was taller than him by a head. I couldn't understand what she saw in him. But then, who could ever understand dames?

He walked swiftly, the dame clattering along beside him, not once looking over his shoulder to make sure I was following. It was a long walk, plunging into darkened backstreets and winding through cobbled alleyways. Finally he stopped outside a dimly-lighted private house, pointed down the basement steps.

'I'll take the dough now,' he said.

'How do I know she's there?'

'I'm telling you.'

'I'll check on it first.'

I clattered down the stone basement steps. He hesitated for a moment indecisively. Then he followed down after me. Dim lights showed through the glass panels of the half-open door. I pushed inside, cat-footed along the dimly-lighted passageway. The place stank. My nose crinkled with the vile stench.

Pokey was right behind me. 'Follow your nose,' he said.

'Straight ahead.'

Straight ahead led me into a big, dimly-lighted room. I stared around and felt sick. The room was filthy, stank abominably of excretion, decaying vegetation and marijuana. It was bare except for the filthy piles of rags set at intervals around the room on the dirt-encrusted floor. Human beings were lying on those piles of rags in various stages of dress and undress. An old, witch-like woman dressed in black sat at a low table, fashioning reefers with crooked, shaking fingers. Her old eyes peered through the dimness toward me, then looked away uninterestedly.

I got a grip on myself, fought off the revulsion inside me and made for the far corner of the room, where a bright red slash of colour against the grey of a filthy heap of rags showed that Pokey had earned his dough.

I stood staring down at her. She'd lost one shoe, her red frock was rolled up around her waist, and her slim white legs looked pathetic, so white and clean against the verminous rags beneath her. She lay on her back with arms outflung and an expression of idyllic tranquillity on her white face.

I bent down, shook her shoulder. It was like trying to wake an unconscious man.

'You're wasting your time,' said Pokey. 'If you wanna get her out of here, you'll have to carry her.'

I glanced up at him. 'What's the matter with her?'

'Needled,' he said briefly and knowingly. He squatted down beside me, his forefinger tracing a pattern on Moira's white thighs. 'Here,' he said, indicating a red pinprick. 'That's fresh. And here. And here!'

The breath whistled out between my teeth. I was wondering how I was gonna keep my hands off him. Because, to me, in that moment, he somehow symbolised the drug racket, the men who live on the misery of others.

'She musta been on short rations,' he judged. 'Needled herself good and proper. Too big a jolt.'

'Yeah,' I said. My fingers were twitching. I was fighting hard to stop myself wrapping them around his neck.

'What about the dough?' he said.

I got out the dough, gave it to him. He stood there, counted it slowly.

'Get out,' I gritted.

'No hurry. I just wanna check …'

'Get out,' I gritted again, and there was murder in my voice. He looked up, startled, saw the expression in my eyes and used his intelligence. He melted away like quicksilver.

I was shaking. If he'd have remained another coupla seconds I'd have killed him. I was sure of it. I took out my handkerchief, wiped my forehead. I put away the handkerchief slowly, drew a deep breath, bent down and picked Moira up in my arms.

The old crone didn't even glance up when I carried Moira from the room and along the corridor. When I got to the top of the basement steps, the street was deserted. Pokey and his dame had disappeared.

I stood Moira on her feet, tried to support her by putting my arm around her waist. But she was out cold, sagging, a limp weight in my arms, impossible to shift unless I carried her.

That's what I had to do. I carried her in my arms like she was a baby through the darkened streets until I found a telephone kiosk.

Rawlins must have been sitting on the other end. He picked up the receiver as soon as the telephone began to ring.

'I've got her,' I panted. 'You can send the car.'

9

When we got her home she was still out cold, breathing softly and with a pleasant smile on her face, as though she was having wonderful dreams.

I put her on the bed, dressed the way she was, pulled a sheet over her. Rawlins watched with worried blue eyes.

I bolted the door of her room, and Lin poured a large whisky for me. Rawlins gestured to him wearily. 'Okay, Lin,' he said. 'Just leave us alone, will ya?'

'I'm sorry,' I told Rawlins humbly. 'I should have been smart enough to ...'

'Forget it,' he interrupted tiredly. He even worked up a weak grin. 'We've got to face up to it, Hank,' he said. 'We can't play with this thing. When she's short of supplies, she's desperate. She'll do anything to get more. We can't do it the easy way. We've got to be tough. We've got to imprison her, find a prison that'll keep her inside and the others out. We've got to find a place where, no matter what happens, she can't get at it.'

'Even in Sing-Sing she'd get supplies,' I said grimly. 'There's always folks ready to peddle the stuff for what they get out of it.'

He looked at me steadily. 'There's only you and me in this room, Hank. I know one place you can take her. You'll both be alone, imprisoned together. But nobody will be able to get at you. And you won't be able to get out to anybody.'

I stared at him levelly. 'If you've got a place like that, I'll take her there.'

He smiled wryly. 'You'll be on your own with her, Hank,' he said. 'Every minute of every day you'll be on your own. You won't see another soul, won't have anyone else to talk to. Whatever trouble crops up, you'll have to handle it yourself. It's a tough proposition. Much tougher than being a guest in my house and looking after her.'

'I'm not crying off,' I said softly.

He crossed the room to the bookcase, pulled out a folded, sectional map. He opened it up on the tabletop. It was a large-scale map of the coast of Florida. His finger traced the coastline then stopped. 'That's where we are,' he said.

'And?'

His forefinger traced another path due south, straight out into the ocean. It stopped, indicating a tiny dot almost lost in the surrounding ocean. 'That's an island,' he said unnecessarily.

My eyes slipped to the scale of miles. I calculated swiftly. 'About eighty miles off the coast?'

'Eighty-seven,' he corrected, and his blue eyes were staring into mine intently. He didn't have to say anything. I knew exactly what was in in his mind.

'What's it like there?' I asked.

He shrugged. 'Pleasant enough. A coupla miles in diameter, beach all the way around, a certain amount of vegetation, a few trees, and … the really important thing … a natural water spring.'

'How do we know we're gonna be alone?'

'It's my island,' he said. 'I bought it. You've seen my yacht. Sometimes when I go fishing, I anchor off there for a coupla days, get fresh water and stretch my legs. But it's well off the fishing lanes. Nobody ever goes that far off course. Additionally, the weather around there's tricky. It blows up quickly, with very heavy seas. My yacht was built to take weather. There's not many folks around who've got a yacht like mine.'

'How do I get her there?'

'That's going to be your first problem. You see, only you and

I have to know about this. If a whisper of it gets beyond us two, you'll get visitors for sure.'

I got up, thoughtfully lit a cigarette and paced the room a coupla times.

'Can I get there with the launch?' I stabbed at him.

'If you can navigate.'

'I know enough,' I grunted.

'You'll be all right,' he said. 'You'll get there. The trouble is, you can carry only enough petrol to make the single journey.'

'You can pick us up in your yacht in two or three weeks' time.'

He thought about it, nodded agreement.

'What's the chance of running into rough weather?' I asked.

'Night time is the best,' he said. 'It rarely blows at night.'

I paced the room some more. 'We'll go tomorrow night,' I told him.

It was his idea. It was for the sake of his daughter. But now he was facing up to it, he was scared. His face was haggard. 'You sure you wanna take this on, Hank?'

I nodded grimly. 'Yeah,' I said. 'I started this thing, I'm gonna see it through. But I want to take off tomorrow evening after dark. And I shall want the launch.'

'You make your own plans.'

'I'll need some dough,' I continued. 'And I'll need some co-operation from you.'

'Anything you say.'

'And right now,' I said heavily, 'I need some sleep. Because tomorrow I'm not gonna get much.'

* * *

She still had that sickly, drug-happy expression on her face when I took in her breakfast Shooting the bolt on her door awakened her. She blinked at me sleepily, stretched herself deliciously and sensuously like a cat lying in the sun, then sat up. The sheet fell down to her waist, and in the light of morning I could see the dirt smears on her red frock.

'Good morning,' I said gruffly.

'Good morning to you,' she said. Her face, voice and poise made her look like a bride waking up after the wedding night, elated by recent pleasures and eager for more. That's one of the difficulties in coping with hopheads. You can never tell what their moods are gonna be.

I poured the coffee, arranged her breakfast on the tray. I became aware she was staring at me. When I glanced up, she was looking at me like she'd never seen me before.

'I'm Moira,' she said, and her eyes were still lingering on me, eager, glinting with intention.

I picked up the tray, thrust it toward her roughly. 'Here,' I grunted. 'Here's your breakfast. You ought to be hungry.' My hands were slippery on the smooth handles.

'It's cute, you getting my breakfast,' she said huskily. She realised she was still dressed, pulled back the sheet, swung her legs around so she was sitting on the edge of the bed. Her creased skirt rode up over her knees. Her eyes flicked artfully to mine to make sure I was noticing it. 'Gee, I'm famished,' she said. 'I musta broken out really good last night.'

I thrust the tray on her lap. 'Eat up,' I grunted sourly.

Her black eyes reflected mock hurt. 'Aw, be nice to me, honey,' she pleaded.

'Eat up,' I grunted. I sat at the table, set the example. She was torn between continuing our discussion and eating. Hunger won. She probably figured she'd have time for talking afterwards. She waded into her breakfast with real appetite. You'd never figure such a slender dame could eat with such lusty vigour.

When she was through, she pushed the tray on one side and concentrated her gaze on me. Her attitude seemed to say, *That's one job finished, now we can start on the other.*

I gulped my coffee quickly, felt the palms of my hands go clammy. I wished she wouldn't keep looking at me that way.

'We've been wasting our time, honey,' she drawled.

'Cut it out,' I rasped.

She lowered her head so she could look at me from beneath

her eyelashes, smiled enigmatically. 'Don't you like me, honey?'

'You're hopped-up,' I told her brutally. 'You're losing control of yourself.'

She gave a husky, sexy sigh. 'I've got a nice figure,' she said invitingly. 'You should see me in evening dress.' Her fingers fumbled at the bodice of her frock, undoing buttons. 'I've got nice shoulders. Everyone says I've got nice shoulders.'

I half rose, stretched out a detaining hand in protest, my palms suddenly slippery and my heart pounding. She was quicker off the mark than me, shrugged the frock off her shoulders so that it fell down her upper arms. I sank back in my chair, powerless. Her modesty was in her own hands, literally in her own hands.

'There!' she said, like seeking my approval. 'Haven't I got nice shoulders?'

She had; soft, white and tempting. And she was playing me now like an angler plays a fish. She knew how I was sweating on account that only her deft fingers held the bodice in place. She had only to release it and it would fall around her waist.

'I like evening dresses,' she said, her black eyes brimming with merriment as she gauged my reactions. 'I like them cut low. Usually, they're as low as this.'

She let the bodice slip a coupla inches, shaped it to herself with deft fingers. I took out my handkerchief, wiped my forehead, tried to look unconcerned and failed miserably.

The black eyes were still laughing, gauging. 'Once I wore one as low as this!'

There was a long pause while she allowed me to examine the daring of that evening dress. I moistened my dry lips, said in a cracked voice: 'It musta been fine. Now I'll clear away …'

The black eyes were frankly inviting. 'I've often wanted to wear one as low as … this!'

My brain was a hot mist. I stumbled to my feet, piled the dishes onto the tray with hands that were four times their normal size. All the time, I was conscious of her sitting there, demonstrative, chuckling huskily and invitingly.

I reached for a cup on the occasional table. It brought me

within reach of her. She moved in on me, urgent and sensuous. She used both hands, and the bodice yielded to the inevitability of gravity.

I clasped her wrists, disentangled her hands from my waist and pushed her back toward the bed. She went backwards easily and eagerly, her hands twisting in mine, grasping my wrists and pulling at me so that only by an effort did I avoid sprawling on top of her.

She lay there, half-reclining, her eyes slumberous and frankly inviting, her arms outspread submissively, her skin soft and marble-white, in marked contrast to the vivid red of her frock draped around her waist. I sensed the warmness of her skin, could see the soft, yielding texture of it, was fascinated by the way her breasts became pointed, gently rounded mounds when she stretched her arms above her head.

There was a buzzing in my head and an uncontrollable desire inside me. It would have been different if she hadn't wanted me. But every fibre of her was screaming out for me. I stood staring down at her, taut like a bowstring. There was sensuous triumph in her black eyes as she moved her body invitingly.

I broke it. It needed just about the biggest effort I've ever made. I broke the tension, the sweat ice-cold on my shoulders, the hammering of my heart seeming like it came from deep down inside a bale of wool. I grabbed the tray, walked quickly toward the door.

She didn't believe it at first, lay there narrow-eyed and acceptive. Then suddenly she sat up, swung her legs off the bed. 'Hank,' she called imperiously. 'Come here.'

I walked on. I was trembling all over. I balanced the tray, got the door half-open.

'Hank,' she called again, and this time there was urgent entreaty in her voice.

I glanced over my shoulder. She was coming after me. But very, very slowly. A change had taken place in her, as though the effort of walking was too much. Her face was yellowy, her eyes black caverns. She stretched her hands toward me. 'Hank,' she wailed, and her legs went rubbery so that she sank to her knees.

I dumped the tray in my room, went back to her. It wasn't the same anymore. She didn't even know she was a woman. She was trembling all over like a nervous horse, and there was no strength in her body. I lifted her in my arms, carried her back to bed, put her down gently. Her black eyes stared into mine, pinpointed and dull. Her mouth was twitching and her fingers shaking so badly that she couldn't have held anything. And the rounded breasts that a few moments ago had seemed so vital, vibrant and fascinating, were yellowy and uninspiring.

'You'll be all right in a minute,' I soothed. 'You'll be okay.'

Her lips twitched. She said through her teeth, 'I've gotta have a shot. Jeezus. I've gotta have a shot.'

'You'll be okay,' I said.

She rolled on her side, fought my restraining hands, clung with desperate, shaking fingers to the edge of the bed while she vomited.

It wasn't pleasant. It made me sick all the way through. But I had a job to do, had to look after her.

I assisted her to lie back on the bed, wiped her face and dabbed at her watering eyes. She was shuddering now like she was shivering with malaria. Her eyes stared into mine without recognition. 'I've gotta have a shot. I've gotta have a shot,' she repeated again and again, and from time to time she tried to struggle out of bed, only to fall back weakly as her strength refused to support her.

I didn't hear Rawlins come in. He spoke from behind me. 'I thought this would happen. She's usually sick after she breaks out.'

I wiped my forehead. 'It hurts to see her this way.'

'It does,' he said drily. He added slowly, 'I'll get Lin to clear up the mess if you'll make her presentable.' There was a slightly hard note in his voice. I understood it when I saw where he was looking.

I lifted one limp arm, thrust it into the sleeve of her frock, pulled it up over her shoulder. I buttoned the frock front, and

Rawlins was watching me with hard blue eyes all the time.

'The striptease was her idea,' I said shortly.

'She's my daughter,' he said.

I rounded on him. 'If you want I should quit, that's okay by me. This isn't an easy set-up. She's a nice kid, she's attractive. The striptease was her idea, and I got nothing but grief outta it.'

His blue eyes stared into my angry ones and then dropped. 'I'm sorry, Hank,' he apologised. 'I guess she's the way folks are when they take drugs.' Then he looked up again quickly. 'But I'm relying on you, Hank. She's entirely in your hands.' He moistened his lips. 'Don't take advantage of her.'

I breathed grimly. 'I told you,' I growled. 'It's gonna be the way you want.'

'She's my daughter,' he said again, in explanation. 'It worries me to think of …'

'Yeah, yeah, yeah,' I said angrily. 'Now get Lin in here, will ya? Get this place cleaned up.'

I supervised Lin while he cleaned the room. Moira drifted off into a kinda fretful sleep. I tucked the coverlet up beneath her chin, sat beside her, reading.

Lunchtime she was still sleeping. It was better that way, so I ate my lunch alone, went back to sit beside her afterwards.

It was late afternoon when she finally awakened. As soon as her eyelids fluttered, her mouth began to twitch. Then her hands began to tremble. She sat up with a start, stared around with frightened eyes and swung her feet off the bed. Her sleep had allowed her to gather strength.

'Hiya, Moira,' I said softly.

Her eyes hunted around, found me. They were black pools, recognition and frenzy gleaming in them. 'I've gotta have a shot,' she pleaded. 'You've gotta help me, Hank. I've gotta have a shot.'

'Listen, honey,' I said patiently. 'I wanna help you, but …'

She spread her hands in front of her, watched their shaking with frightened eyes. Her mouth kept twitching, causing her whole cheek to pucker. 'Give me a shot,' she pleaded. 'Just one little shot. That's all I want.'

'It's for your own good, Moira,' I said patiently. 'You see ...'

'I'll give you anything you want,' she pleaded frantically. Memory must have been strong inside her. Her hands went to her frock, jerked savagely, shredding buttons and baring white skin. She thrust herself toward me, a tantalising offering. 'Just a little shot, Hank. You can have anything you want.'

I got up quickly, fought her off. As she trailed after me, I thrust her back into the room, bolted the door behind me. I was sweating again, and I figured I had plenty of reason.

* * *

After it was dark, Rawlins relieved me. I found my way to the landing stage, looked enviously at Rawlins' large yacht moored a quarter of a mile off the coast and climbed aboard his launch.

I ran down the coast toward town, grounded the launch on the deserted, darkened beach a coupla miles lower down. Then I walked back to the house, got Rawlins' car and drove into town.

I was quiet and as unobtrusive as I knew how. I bought tinned food, biscuits, chocolate and bottled fruit. When I got back to the launch, which was concealed in the darkness, it took an hour to load it with the goods and provisions I'd bought. Then I filled the tanks to capacity with petrol I'd brought in cans in the boot of the car.

I drove the car to the house, walked back to the launch and described a large circle out to sea before I steered the vessel back to the landing stage.

'How's it going?' asked Rawlins, when I got back.

'Everything's ready,' I told him. 'Nobody even knows the launch is provisioned. The next stage is up to you.' I went into it in detail, told him exactly what to do.

Then I checked on Moira. Still the face-twitch and still the trembling hands. In her half-crazed mind had blossomed some crazy association of me, desire and drugs. She didn't get up when I entered, remained seated in her chair with her back toward me. But when I got close, she twisted out of the chair like an eel, wrapped her arms around me, pressed herself against me hard. She was still wearing that red frock. It gaped open to the waist. 'I've gotta have it, Hank,' she urged. 'I've gotta have it.'

The way she was holding me, I couldn't tell whether it was drugs or the other thing she wanted. I tried to twist away, but she clung like a limpet. I'd have to use savage force to break her grip.

'It's for your own good, honey,' I said patiently. 'You want to get better, don't you?'

The black eyes stared at me pleadingly. The bodice gaped so wide that bare flesh was nudging me hard. Her arms were straining her toward me with an incredible strength. She moved her body subtly, irresistibly. 'You've gotta let me have it, Hank,' she half-moaned. 'Can't you see? I'll go crazy. I've gotta have it.'

It was like it had been before, only ten times stronger. Because before, she'd lain back on the bed, inviting and submissive. Now she was aggressive. She wasn't leaving it to me: she was taking the initiative.

There was a hot red mist pounding in my head, my hands were sweaty and itchy and I was slipping, slipping, slipping! I didn't know what was happening. It was all so natural, so easy, so inevitable. And then she whispered hoarsely, 'I've got to have it first, Hank. Give me a shot before we ...'

If she hadn't spoken, anything mighta happened. But her words broke the spell. They were a sudden blinding glare of light through the utter darkness. I made a superhuman effort, pushed her away from me.

Her black eyes were wide, incredulous. Then they gleamed with savage determination. She moved in on me quickly, determinedly, and at the same time she was tugging her frock down around her upper arms

I know when I'm beat. I'd slipped until I was on the brink, tottering on the edge about to plunge into the depths. The determined way she moved in on me, her obvious intention and undoubted allure, all had me beat. If she got near enough to touch me ...

I turned and ran. A tiny corner of my brain still exercising cool reasoning told me flight was my only hope. Yeah, I ran like a terrified schoolkid desperate to escape an avenger. I got out of the room, slammed the door, shot the bolts home. I leaned against the door, breathing heavily, trying to simmer down.

Rawlins asked anxiously, 'She's making trouble?'

I stared at him. 'Yeah,' I said absently, and I was remembering the plan: two of us alone together for a fortnight; my sole companion Moira, who would try every way to get her hands on drugs. Then there was Rawlins, dependent upon me, trusting me to remember that Moira was his daughter.

'Better get yourself a drink,' he advised.

I crossed to the cabinet, poured myself a drink. My hand was trembling, I was panting, and the memory of her white body kept shimmering into my brain.

'You sure it's the best way to do it?' he asked.

'It's the best way,' I assured him. 'Everybody will think she's made a getaway. That's fine. The pedlars will sit around waiting for her to turn up instead of trying to find her.'

'I just hope it works,' he said sincerely.

I finished my drink. 'I'm going out,' I said abruptly. 'I'm going downtown for a coupla hours.'

He stared at me. 'Something you've forgotten? I can send somebody ...'

'It's something I've gotta do,' I gritted.

'What's so important it has to be done now, at this time!'

Quite unreasonably I got angry. 'What's it to you?' I almost yelled. 'I've got business. That's good enough, ain't it?'

His blue eyes were startled. 'That's good enough for me,' he said quietly, reprovingly. 'You can take my car.'

I growled, brushed out of the room without a word of explanation.

* * *

I knew Jane would be halfway through her sale of lottery tickets. But it wasn't her I was wanting to see when I knocked at the door of the boarding-house and encountered the frosty gaze of the sharp-faced, scrawny-necked landlady.

'He's on the second floor,' she told me, her sharp eyes weighing me up, wondering who I was and what my business could be. She stood at the foot of the stairs, her sharp eyes following me as I ascended. When I took the second flight, she craned her neck to watch me through the staircase well.

I knocked at the door, pushed it open and walked in. 'Hiya, John,' I said, and tossed my fedora onto the nearest chair.

He was sitting at the work table, tools at his side and a subdued blow-lamp waiting to be put in use.

His fair head jerked up, his grey eyes widened and then he smiled a welcome. 'Come right in, fella,' he greeted. 'This sure is a surprise.'

I flashed a glance at my wristwatch, said abruptly, 'We know each other, John. We'll cut the preliminaries. I want to commission you. I want you to do a job for me right away. It's urgent. I've got to have it tonight.'

His eyes showed his surprise. But he didn't waste time arguing. He said, 'What's the job?'

'Pencil and paper,' I demanded.

He told me where to get them. I'm no artist, but I knew what I wanted. I drew a rough outline, described to him in detail exactly what I had in mind His eyes widened, stared at me in astonishment.

'What the hell d'you want a thing like that for?'

'You can do it, huh?'

His eyes calculated. 'Take a coupla hours, maybe longer. Even if you help me, that is.'

'Let's get cracking then, fella,' I suggested. 'Tell me what I have to do.'

His eyes were still astonished. 'What do you use a thing like that for?'

I flushed. 'Be a good guy, will ya?' I pleaded. 'Quit asking questions. This is kinda personal.'

He shrugged. 'Okay, it's your say-so. You're the customer.' He looked at my drawing, narrowed one eye as he calculated, and said, 'Over there in that corner. Find a strip of copper about a quarter of an inch thick. There's a hacksaw here. Cut it two feet long and one inch wide.'

'Sure, boss,' I grinned, and made for the corner.

We worked desperately hard, sweating in the Florida evening heat. I did the rough work. He concentrated on the delicate mechanism, the complicated lock. It was incredible to me how, beneath his fingers, it began to take shape. It wasn't a work of art. It didn't have to be. It had use value, not artistic value.

We worked, sweated, twisted, hammered and cut. And finally it was assembled, the pieces rivetted firmly together, dovetailing perfectly and smoothly. I stood back, eyed it with satisfaction.

'That's fine,' I said. 'Just what I want.'

He looked at it, he looked at me. 'Maybe it is,' he said, doubtfully. 'What the hell is it?'

I flushed again. The last thing I wanted was to tell anyone what it was for. I changed the subject abruptly. 'You've got two keys?'

'Both here.' He offered them to me.

I took one. 'I want you to keep the other. I'll be along for it sometime. Whatever you do, don't lose it.'

He shrugged, looked at me as though I was crazy. 'Just as you wish.'

I glanced at my watch again. I had another worry now. Jane would be back at any time. I didn't want her to see me. I didn't want her to see that article either. I had the uneasy feeling she'd sense what it was. I found my original drawing, ripped it into pieces. I found an old newspaper, wrapped up the article. Then I argued with him about payment. He wanted to take only a workman's pay. I wanted to pay him for the job. Finally he agreed, he accepting what seemed too much and me paying what seemed too little.

'I'll be seeing you again, John,' I told him.

'Pity you can't wait to see Jane. I'll give her your best wishes.'

'And thanks a million,' I added.

'When will you be around again?'

I took a deep breath, forced a grin. 'Two or three weeks, maybe.'

He shook his head sadly, but his eyes smiled with merriment. 'Shan't sleep tonight,' he said.

'Something on your mind?'

'Sure,' he said. 'Trying to figure out what you're gonna use that for.'

'If only you knew, brother!' I said heavily. 'If only you knew!'

10

By 12 o'clock, Moira had passed almost twenty-four hours without a sniff of a drug. Nearly all day she'd been suffering a physical reaction, facial twitchings, the trembling of hands and convulsive shudders. Shortly after I got back, the emotional strain proved too much for her. Rawlins, white-faced, sat listening with me to her anguished pleadings the other side of the door, her nails tearing at the panels and her tearful entreaties eating right down inside us.

Rawlins' face was haggard. 'I can't stand it any longer, Hank,' he said.

'You know what to do.'

He nodded. 'Sure,' he said. 'I know what to do.' I was scared he wouldn't be able to carry through with it.

I got up. 'I'll be seeing you,' I said.

He got up slowly, stretched out to shake my hand. 'Best of luck, Hank,' he said huskily. 'It's all up to you.'

'Let's hope it works,' I said.

As soon as I'd left the room, he rang for Lin. Lin came in, his smooth, boyish face registering just a trace of surprise. He appeared not to notice the heart-rending wails of Moira the other side of that bolted door.

Rawlins drew himself up, kinda squared his shoulders. 'I want you to help me, Lin,' he said. 'My daughter should be in bed. Help me persuade her, will you?'

Another momentary glimpse of surprise showed in Lin's

eyes. That was all. Obediently he moved toward the door, Rawlins right behind him.

They got the door open, and Moira was on them, face contorted as she screeched wildly, hands clawing and feet kicking. She was still wearing that red frock, more off than on. Lin's face was impassive as he wrapped his arms around her, struggled with Rawlins to drag her to the bed. In the scuffle, Rawlins didn't seem to notice he'd left the door open. Moira did. Suddenly she relaxed, went limp so that it needed their combined efforts to carry her. They put her on the bed, Rawlins talking to her soothingly the whole time. She lay quiet, black eyes staring emotionlessly at the ceiling. Rawlins said, 'I think she's quietened down. If she could have a sedative, a glass of milk and a sleeping tablet? You'll see to that, will you, Lin?'

Lin nodded obediently, slipped away swiftly. Moira said weakly, 'I feel faint. Get me my smelling salts, will you? They're on my dressing table.'

It was obvious, but Rawlins seemed to fall for it. He was still at the dressing table, looking for the smelling salts, when she slipped from the bed like an eel, ran desperately and barefooted from the room, even being smart enough to slam and bolt the door behind her so that Rawlins was imprisoned on the inside.

It was Lin's unlucky day. He knew nothing of the plan, and when he returned bearing a glass of milk and saw the wild-eyed Moira sprinting along the corridor toward him, he did his duty as he saw fit, dropped the tray and grappled with her.

He had the disadvantage all men have when grappling with dames. He had the savage strength to overpower her but didn't want to use it. Moira, on the other hand, knew no scruples, only a desperate desire to get her hands on life-giving drugs. As Lin grappled with her, she used subtlety, relaxed in his arms. When, as a result, he handled her more gently, she wrenched herself loose with a savage jerk, picked up the nearest thing to hand – a big earthenware vase – and smashed it savagely on his head.

The blow was merciless. It drove Lin to his knees, with blood pouring down across his forehead into his eyes. One jagged piece of broken vase cut a semicircle of flesh from his skull that could be lifted up and down like a flap and would need six stitches.

But Moira knew or thought nothing of this. Her one desperate aim was escape to town. Her feet barely touched the ground as she continued her flight along the passage, wrenched open the door of the study, ran across the room to the French windows. The white sand was silver in the moonlight. She ran like a wood-nymph, sand spurting from her bare feet as, with eager, anticipating eyes, she raced toward the launch.

Rawlins had a private stone jetty built out into the sea. The launch was moored at the end, in deep water. Her bare feet padded swiftly along the stone jetty, her breathing laboured as she bent to release the hawsers.

Even that action showed she was thinking quickly. She didn't stay moored while she got the engine running; she cast off, pushed away, leaving an ever-expanding stretch of water between the launch and the jetty before she started it.

She hadn't a thing to worry about. The engine was in perfect condition, started first time. As soon as it got moving, she notched it up to top speed, set the nose toward the bright lights of the fairground.

She was halfway there, preparing to turn in and run the launch up onto the sand, when I climbed out from under the tarpaulin in the well of the launch.

She stood at the wheel, oblivious to everything, her face white and set and her eyes straining ahead, as though she could already smell the scent of the life-giving drug for which she craved.

I hadn't come unprepared. She had no idea I was there until I dropped the loop of rope over her head. It slid down around her waist, clamping her arms to her sides as I pulled on it tightly. She gave a gasp of surprise and then, animal-like, began to struggle ferociously and instinctively.

As I've said, I hadn't come unprepared. The rope held her long enough to enable me to slip the long canvas bag over her head, draw it down over her shoulders and around her waist. I pulled the rope taut at the neck of the bag, fastened it securely around her waist, tying the loose end of the rope to a bollard on the side of the launch. I tied it so she could stand or sit as she pleased, yet not have the run of the boat.

The launch was roaring in toward the beach now, the helm unattended. I swung it in a wide arc, headed out to sea. I knew my exact position, knew the course I should take. I set the boat dead on course, fixed the helm and went back to Moira.

She wasn't lying down under this treatment. Her muffled voice was frantic and she struggled desperately. Her arms and hands were completely enveloped in that canvas bag, which rendered them useless. But she'd worked the bag up from around her waist to just below her breasts.

I'd tied that bag tightly. She wasn't likely to get it any higher. I dug down into the well of the boat, found a straw mattress and spread it out for her, took her by the shoulders and forced her down onto it. She sat down heavily, not able to use her arms to aid herself.

'Take it easy, honey,' I soothed. 'You won't get anywhere this way.'

Talking was a mistake. It gave her a direction. Her bare heel smashed my lips against my teeth. I staggered away from her, spitting blood, and with an angry *I-don't-care-what-happens-to-you* feeling.

It seemed she didn't either. Somehow, she staggered to her feet, bracing herself against the roll of the launch, and tried to go head-first over the side into the sea. I was almost tempted to let her do it, wait till she was half drowned before I hauled her in again. I grabbed her by the shoulders, pulled her away from the side. She tried to butt me under the chin with her head. I sighed wearily, hooked my foot behind her ankles, jerked her feet away so that she sat down hard on the mattress. While she was recovering from that, I found another length of rope, looped it around one threshing ankle and secured the other end to a bollard on the other side of the launch. The only way she wouldn't spend the rest of the journey sitting or lying on the mattress would be if she was able to stand on one leg without the use of her arms.

She tried it. She sure had determination. She tried it more than a dozen times before she gave it up. Finally, realising it was hopeless, she lay back on the mattress. Muffled sobs came from beneath the canvas bag.

I lit a cigarette, went up to the bows of the launch. There was a gentle swell and the launch rolled as it churned through the water, a milk-white crescent rising from the bow and an expanding wedge of moon-flecked foam spreading behind us. Already the lights of the coast were out of sight, and I judged we must be five or six miles off the coast, with another eighty miles of open sea before us.

It was a warm Florida night. The spray was salty and cooling. There was no wind and the roar of the engine was the only sound in this silver-flecked, moonlit world. It was gonna be a long journey. I settled down to it philosophically.

It got cooler later. I put on a jacket and looked at Moira thoughtfully. She was lying so still I wasn't sure if she was asleep. Her skirt was rucked high up over her thighs and there was nothing she could do about it. I pulled down her skirt and discovered she was awake. Her knee scrunched against my jaw. I muttered harsh things beneath my breath, mentally condemned her to death by freezing, but finally relented. I dug down under the tarpaulin at the back of the boat, fished out a blanket.

I covered her with it. She kicked it off. I covered her with it. She kicked it off. I covered her with it. She kicked it off …

An hour later it was distinctly chilly. I turned up the collar of my jacket, pulled it close around my neck. I spread the blanket over her again, tucked it in. This time there was no kicking. She was learning sense.

I had a thermos flask full of hot coffee. I laced it with whisky, drank it slowly and felt it warming my belly. I would have liked to give Moira some. But it would have meant releasing her. Coping with Moira in an open speed-launch in the middle of the ocean was something I didn't feel up to.

It seemed coldest when dawn began to break. I saw the horizon begin to lighten, become a rosy glow. Then a thin crescent of sun edged above the blue line of the sea. It was a glorious dawn. I stood with feet astride, braced against the sway of the throbbing launch, watching the giant, life-giving orb emerge from its resting place. I could feel the warmth from it, golden rays stabbing across the blue sea, turning the white cream at the bows of the launch into glistening, golden froth.

It was the right moment to take a bearing. I checked the map, checked my position, and found I was half a degree off course. I corrected the deviation, took the wheel manually and rejoiced in the fresh morning air.

The sea was vast, stretching as far as the eye could see and deeper than man could ever know. The launch was a tiny speck upon that vast ocean. Yet, slowly and surely, with instruments devised by man, that tiny speck approached inevitably, that tiny oasis of land pinpointed on the map.

I was alone in a vast world of sea and sky. It was exhilarating. I sang aloud as the boat rolled beneath my feet and the floorboards throbbed with the steady, rhythmic power of mighty engines. Out of the night and into the dawn, that small launch creamed its way at top speed, rhythmic pistons pounding and sucking the contents of the petrol tank, drawing life from it as I drew life from the sun.

It was a magnificent morning. When, at long last, far ahead where sea met sky, I saw a tiny smudge, my heart leaped. I thrilled with a sense of achievement at having brought the launch and its cargo across this expanse of sea to hit my objective head-on.

The launch was still travelling at top speed. Slowly, incredibly slowly, we drew nearer to the island. From a distance it looked bare and uninviting. As we got closer I could see the white sands and the vivid green of flowering palm trees. Then it seemed we were approaching the island much faster, it was expanding, opening out like a baseball ground on television when the telescopic sights rush you down to a close-up.

I geared down the engine, kept the bows pointed at the beach. Our speed dropped off but we were still going fast when the bows creamed through shallow water, rushed up onto the beach, stranding the launch like a seal, coming to a standstill so abruptly that I was jolted forward.

Well, this was it. I switched off the engine, opened the housing and removed the distributor. I concealed it beneath the engine base. Then I checked the petrol. There was maybe a coupla gallons left. I syphoned it out with a rubber tube, let it drain over the side into the sea, leaving the tank as dry as a bone. The launch was grounded so far up on the beach that it'd take six strong men to get it floating again. Moira was tough, but I didn't think she was tough enough to swim eighty-five miles. So there wasn't any reason I could see why she shouldn't be released.

I loosened the neck of the canvas bag, stood back and watched her as she pulled it off. Her eyes were angry and desperate. But her face was white, the twitch of her lips much more pronounced, and her hands trembly. So trembly that it took her all her time to release the rope I'd tied around her ankle.

She clawed herself to her feet, stared around with horror growing in her eyes. 'Where are we?' she panted. 'Where have you brought me?'

I made no bones about it. 'We're eighty-five miles off the coast of Florida. Nobody ever comes here. We're here until you get better. And this is one place where you won't get any supplies.'

She stared at me, and her lips writhed, showing keen white teeth. 'You're crazy,' she screamed. 'You can't keep me here. I won't let you. You can't do it.'

I shrugged my shoulders, ignored her, started shifting the provisions from the well of the launch up into the bows. She sat on the edge of the launch, watching me with hate-filled eyes that were cunning and calculating.

I ignored her, jumped from the bows of the boat onto the sand and loaded myself with the first armful of stores.

It was such a small island that you could take in its total size at a glance. The beach was fine white sand extending up toward sparse undergrowth on rocky soil. It was an unimaginative island, smoothly formed like a giant hummock. The centre of it, which was the highest point, wasn't more than two hundred feet above sea level.

I shouldered the stores, walked up toward one of the palm trees. In the shade of this tree would be the best place to make camp. I reached it, unloaded myself and returned to the launch for more.

Moira was out of sight. But I knew where she was. The engine-housing was open and the electric starter was whirring like mad as she pressed it desperately, hoping the engine would fire.

'You're wasting your time,' I called aloud. 'Even if the engine worked, there's no petrol.'

She musta realised the truth of what I said, because when I got back to the boat for my third armful of provisions she was red in the face with the exertion of trying to run the launch single-handed into the water. She had as much chance of moving that launch as I have of pushing over the Woolworth buildings with my bare hands.

The next time I looked to see what she was doing, she was running along the beach, glancing desperately from side to side, as though seeking something that would offer her hope. I let her run. The island was small. She couldn't get lost. And if she kept running the way she was now, in no time she'd be back where she started.

11

I had plenty to keep me busy, and I wanted to do it before the sun got too high. I erected three small tents, loaded the centre one with supplies of tinned food, eating implements, books and cigarettes. I spread groundsheets in the other two tents, placed folded blankets ready for use. I stood up, surveyed my work with satisfaction. This was to be our home for the next two or three weeks. It would be comfortable enough, even if the conditions were a little primitive.

The sun was beating through my shirt onto my back. There wasn't any point in wasting it. I stripped off my shirt, picked up a two-gallon water jar and started off through the sun-dried undergrowth, up to the summit of the mound, where I'd find the spring.

In the hot sun it was a steep climb. Yet it was worth it. From there, I had a view of the entire island. I shaded my eyes, followed the path Moira had taken along the beach. I saw her at last, a bright red fleck of colour against the white beach, stooping, moving with a sudden swift little dart and then stooping again. It was too far to see what she was doing. But whatever it was, it wasn't gonna help her get dope.

I went back to the spring. It was maybe a coupla feet deep. Tiny bubbles sparkled to the surface as water bubbled up from deep down in the ground.

I scooped water to my lips. It was sweet and clean-tasting. I poured it over my head and felt refreshed. Then I filled the jar, hoisted it to my shoulder, went back to the camp.

It was an ideal place to spend a holiday, if you didn't have worries. Moira was on my mind. But I knew the difficulty I had with her now was nothing to what I'd have later. It would be a good plan to relax whenever I got the chance. The chance was right now.

I climbed into my bathing trunks, lazed in the sun, and when it got too hot, ran into the sea.

It was pleasant there if you wanted to be lazy. I did. I dried off in the sun, lay in the shadow of the palm tree with a book, cigarettes and an opened bottle of beer.

There was the murmur of the surf, the silent heaviness of sun-laden air and a sleepless night to soothe me. I was soothed. I fell asleep.

I musta slept for hours, awakening drowsily to the soft murmur of the surf and the hum of a busy insect. I propped myself on my elbow, drained the half-empty beer bottle, stretched and climbed to my feet.

I was hungry. It was way past lunchtime. Moira musta been hungry too. It worried me she wasn't around.

I'd already discovered that the summit of the island was an ideal look-out. I climbed up there, the sun hot on my back and a heat haze causing the ground to shimmer.

She was still there, had worked her way three-quarters around the island. The way she acted, she was searching for something. I went down after her. The closer I got, the more she reminded me of an animal, a dog rooting for food in the garbage-cans. When I got real close, I stood and stared at her. She was on hands and knees, searching feverishly in the dried scrub and bushes, scrambling from one to another, plucking berries and dried pods, snuffling at them, biting them and spitting them out in disgust. Instinctively I felt what she was after. She was in the grip of the craving, was searching the island like an animal, snuffling, biting and smelling at every plant in the desperate hope she could find a substitute to satisfy the overwhelming desire inside her.

I moved closer still, got between her and the sun, sent my

shadow leaping across the ground in front of her. She spun around, startled, her teeth bared and her black eyes wild and desperate. She looked dangerous, like a wild animal at bay, not only ready but able to rend and tear my throat.

'You must be hungry, Moira,' I said gently. 'How about some food, huh?'

She snarled, spat like a cat with its back arched. Somehow, with her red frock torn at the front, soiled and creased, she didn't seem human.

'You've gotta eat, Moira,' I said gently. 'Let's go, huh?'

She spat, snarled some more.

I moved in on her, slowly, carefully. She backed, still snarling, lips writhing back from her bared teeth, one hand upraised to slash with red, pointed nails. She broke first, turned, ran from me like a hunted animal, her bare feet dusty and bleeding from the rough ground. When she had placed a fair distance between us, she crouched low over a bush, went on all fours, snuffling and chewing like an animal, while all the time her black eyes were watching me, allowing me to approach only so near before she scampered in front of me again, rooted at another bush.

By walking slowly that way, I herded her around the island back to our camp. She rooted among the bushes at a discreet distance, watching me suspiciously, like a cat watches a dog, while I lit a fire, prepared lunch.

I chose tinned bacon and beans. The smell of it sizzling over the wood fire was so delicious, I felt pained with hunger. The smell reached Moira. She raised her head, and I saw her nostrils quiver. But it might have been burning rubber for all the interest she took in it.

I ate her share as well as my own. I washed it down with bottled beer. I poured water into a mug, went as near to her as she would allow, set down the mug and retreated to a safe distance. The craving musta been strong inside her. She didn't even realise she was thirsty.

I watched her closely after that, sat smoking, followed after her when she got too far away. She was inexhaustible, scrambling untiringly from bush to bush in that hot sun. As the day wore on, she became more desperate, rooting along the beach, burrowing the sand away from rocks as though there was no avenue of hope she was willing to leave unexplored.

I tried to understand how she was feeling, what she was thinking. Maybe she wasn't a thinking human being anymore? Her physical system had been gradually accustomed to more and more dope and was now consumed by a physical craving that extinguished her mind. Her brain was overwhelmed by the craving, her body nothing but a physical driving desire. She was behaving like an animal, probably had the primaeval instincts of an animal.

It was toward evening, when the sun was setting, that she suffered a reaction. She was scrabbling beneath a rock like a dog, scooping sand with her hands, spattering it around her in a fine shower. Suddenly she stopped, sat back on her heels, took a deep breath and then began to howl.

It was terrible to hear her. It was like the howling of a wildly-tormented animal. It was hell to listen to. She kept it up for maybe ten minutes, then rolled on her side, scrabbled at the sand, kicking with her feet like she was in torment.

It was hell to watch her. It was like seeing a child suffering and being unable to do anything about it. All I could do was sweat and tense myself to move in quickly if she started to do herself physical injury.

She staggered to her feet, reeled in a crazy half-circle, did some more howling and tugged at her hair. Then her feverishly-twitching fingers found the material of the dress, ripped it with a kinda fiendish savagery.

There was a demon burning inside her. The expression on her face became menacing exultation as the material ripped between her fingers. Here was something she could destroy, use to ease the turmoil of emotions inside her.

She didn't merely strip off the frock, she worried it like a dog, tore at it with teeth and hands. She rolled in the sand, ripped and ripped again. The frock became a tattered rag and then tattered fragments. She held pieces between her strong teeth, ripped and tore as long as there was a piece large enough to tear.

I hadn't exactly expected this, but I wasn't surprised. She hadn't been wearing anything beneath that frock. Now, as she crouched there in the sand with red strips of material dripping from her jaws and her black eyes glowing wildly, she was as naked as the day she was born.

She spat the last fragments from her mouth, sat back on her haunches, stared around with a wild, lost look. Her chest heaved as she breathed deeply, and the setting sun transformed her white skin into a coppery glow. I waited, watched, wondered what happened next.

You can never beat nature. She'd been without food or water all day, all the time engaged in tireless movement beneath a hot sun. The savage efforts of the last few moments had exhausted her already-weakened body. She climbed to her feet unsteadily, rivetted her eyes on a rock that she hadn't yet burrowed beneath, stumbled toward it. Halfway there her legs buckled beneath her. Her eyes were still fastened on the rock, and even though she was falling, she didn't seem to realise it, made no effort to save herself, sprawled in the soft sand with one hand outstretched in front of her.

I ran to her. She made a supreme effort, got to her knees, got one foot on the ground and toppled forward again. This time she lay still, eyes closed but mumbling incoherently to herself.

I had a strange, joyous feeling overcome me then, a kinda wonderful feeling. I'd seen her, imagined the kinda dame she could be without the curse of this craving. Right then I felt I was waging a battle for her life, fighting for her against her wishes, fighting a grim battle that was psychologically gonna be a bigger strain on me than any other job I'd tackled.

I bent down, picked her up in my arms. She was a limp, dead weight, thoroughly exhausted, lacking the strength or willpower to look into my face. Her head hung, her long black hair brushed against my thigh, her arms trailed limply, and she was a dead weight. So heavy, I wondered if I'd have the strength to carry her back to camp without resting.

Sure, I know it. She was as naked as the day she was born, and she was in my arms. But it didn't mean a thing to me. I was like a doctor, battling for her life. I didn't think of her as a woman, only as somebody who had to be saved. Yet, as I plodded through the soft sand, I couldn't help noticing her, the slim roundness of her thighs, the tiny crease of flesh around her waist as she sagged in my arms. It was an emotionless, dispassionate scrutiny, the observance of those things not usually revealed and, therefore, of interest to me for that reason only.

It musta been half a mile, and I carried her the whole way without stopping once. I pulled a blanket from the tent, laid her on it gently and placed a pillow for her head. Her head rolled limply to one side and her lips moved as she muttered unintelligible sentences. I poured a mug of water, laced it with whisky and held it to her lips. They should have been warm, moist and inviting. Instead, they were white, dry and scaly. At first she tried to twist her head away. Then, as water seeped into her mouth, her hands reached up instinctively, grasped at the mug urgently, and she gulped greedily. I let her have it a little at a time. When the last drop trickled between her lips, she was staring at me with those black eyes.

'Like some more?'

'I'm hungry,' she said.

It was like she'd been unconscious all day and was now returning to sanity.

'Interested in fried bacon?'

She screwed up her forehead. 'I feel so weak,' she said faintly. 'I'm so hungry.'

I stirred the embers of the fire, found the frying pan and cooked more bacon. She lay still the whole time, moving only her head, her arms limp at her sides. She was so weak that she couldn't lift her head. I had to feed her slowly, a little at a time, waiting patiently while she chewed, knowing that even chewing was an effort almost beyond her.

I cooked more bacon for myself, brewed hot coffee. I laced her mug of coffee with more whisky. When she'd got that down inside her, hot and burning, it gave her fresh strength.

I lit a cigarette, sat beside her, watching her patiently. Slowly, and with an effort, she turned on her side, lay facing me, black eyes staring into mine.

'You're Hank, aren't you?' she said.

'That's right,' I said. 'You're Moira.'

'I feel bad,' she said. She half propped herself up, sat poised like she was wanting to be sick and then eased herself down on the pillow again.

'You know what's the matter with me, don't you?' she asked. It was amazing to hear her speaking so lucidly after what had happened.

'Sure,' I said. 'You caught a touch of sunstroke.'

There was expression in her eyes now, tender appreciation. 'It's through not having the drug, isn't it?' she said simply.

'You're doing fine,' I said encouragingly. 'It's gonna be tough, I know. In a few days more it won't bother you. It'll be out of your system.'

'I know it's for my own good,' she said quietly. Her lip began to twitch and she reached up with her fingers, tried to stop it. 'Where are we, Hank?'

'Marooned,' I said. 'More than eighty miles off the coast of Florida.'

She was thinking that over. 'How will we get away?' she asked cautiously.

'Your father will pick us up.'

'How long do we have to wait?'

I shrugged my shoulders. 'Two or three weeks. Maybe more.'

She'd been pumping me. When she realised how hopeless her position was, the change was startling. Those black eyes registered loathing and hatred. Her lips writhed and her sharp teeth parted, ready to sink into and rend at flesh. 'You did this,' she gasped. 'You're responsible for this suffering.' She was so weak that her sharp movement toward me failed before it started. Her head dropped onto the pillow, her eyes closed and she moaned softly.

'You ought to sleep,' I advised. 'You've exhausted yourself.'

'I want to sleep,' she droned, almost soundlessly.

I went to the supply tent, unearthed a bottle of sleeping tablets. I poured more coffee, laced it with whisky and supported her head while she drank it and swallowed the pills.

'You'll feel better now.'

'I just want to sleep,' she said faintly.

She went off to sleep quickly, even snoring in a ladylike way. I went into her tent, prepared her blankets, carried her inside and covered her with another blanket. She didn't murmur when I moved her, was in a deep sleep of exhaustion.

The sun was completely down by this time. I built up the fire, sat beside it and read. I was still wearing my bathing trunks, and even though I was already brown, exposure to the hot sun for just one day caused my skin to tingle. I was souped up like a battery that's been over-charged. Sitting beside the fire I found it difficult to concentrate on reading. My thoughts kept wandering. Now it was all over, now Moira was asleep, neatly tucked up in the blankets, I kept thinking of the way I'd carried her to the camp, the touch of her soft skin against me as I'd held her in my arms, the smoothness of her skin and the womanly softness of her young, ripe breasts.

I hurled the book away from me, angrily strode up and down the beach. It didn't make me feel any better. I half-filled a mug with whisky, diluted it only a little and used it to wash down a sleeping tablet. Then I climbed into my tent, pulled the blankets over me.

It wasn't any use. Because although I dreamed a lot, I didn't sleep a wink.

12

She crawled out of her tent the next morning while I was frying the sausages. It was a low tent and she came out on hands and knees, her long black hair hanging across her forehead and her face startlingly white. She looked wild - like an animal. What made it worse was the way one side of her face twitched convulsively, the whole cheek moving, drawing down the corner of her mouth and eye. She was panting too, like a sweating dog with its tongue hanging out. She remained on hands and knees, kinda stalked around the campfire, watching me with black, enigmatic eyes and staring hungrily at the frying-pan.

'How d'you feel?' I asked.

She lay on her side, stared at me, then stared at the frying sausages. Of all the people on the island, she was the only one unconscious of her nakedness. I tried not to look at her, shovelled hot sausages onto an enamel plate, passed it to her.

She ate like an animal, using both hands, thrusting food into her mouth, smearing her face with grease that dripped from the point of her chin to her breasts. When she was through eating, she wiped greasy hands on the bare flesh of her belly.

She was a nice kid with a nice figure. But right then she didn't look so hot. With good reason. She hadn't washed in days. Right now, her black hair was unkempt, dried by the sun and full of sand. Her hands and legs were grimed where she'd grovelled in the dry earth, and her feet were dirty and black with congealed blood from tiny scratches. She wasn't a pleasant breakfast-mate.

'Coffee?' I asked.

She didn't say anything, just watched my hands as I picked up the coffee pot, slopped coffee into a mug. When I offered her the mug, she snatched at it, gulped at it greedily, drank it down scalding hot. When she was through, without a word she dropped the mug, climbed to her feet and stumbled off along the beach, like she had somewhere to go that was important.

I watched her with hurt deep down inside me. This was just the beginning. Later it was gonna get worse. I was wondering just how bad it was gonna get, and just what Rawlins would find when he came to relieve us.

I washed up, collected more wood for the fire and swam. A coupla times I climbed to the vantage point on top of the mound and checked on Moira. She was still searching around, hunting like there just had to be what she was looking for.

Like an animal, she turned up again at eating time. She approached stealthily, keeping a distance between us, as though she was scared I was gonna attack her. She approached warily, crouched the opposite side of the campfire and stared at me watchfully. When I offered her food on a plate, she reached for it timidly, then snatched at it, scrambled away to a safe distance and ate it squatting on her haunches, scooping it into her mouth with bare hands as though frightened I'd try to take it from her. It was tinned pork and beans, with plenty of gravy.

I offered her beer, water or coffee. She didn't answer, but her eyes wandered to the beer bottle. I opened it, offered it to her. Once again she approached timidly, snatched swiftly and scampered away with it. She drank greedily and noisily, overfilling her mouth so that it trickled over her chin in a steady flow, rivulets of beer tracing a pattern that reached her thighs. She threw the bottle to one side carelessly, shot me a cautious glance as though still scared I'd attack her, and once again set off along the beach.

The pity was strong inside me. But there was a nausea too. It was getting so I couldn't think of her as a human being, couldn't get from my mind the mental picture of her feeding noisily and dirtily, using her hands and careless that her body should be smeared with the food. Maybe what made it seem worse was her nakedness. She was as unconscious of it as an animal of its pelt.

Maybe the nausea inside me was stronger than the pity. Maybe that's why I read, lazed in the sun, swam and neglected to check on Moira often enough. A coupla hours must have elapsed since the last time I'd checked when I experienced a twinge of worry, began searching the island from my lookout point with mounting uneasiness.

I couldn't see her. And that was crazy because, just by making a small detour around the summit, every part of the island could be raked by the human eye.

I drew a deep breath, checked a second time, looking not just for the movement of her white body but – in case she had burrowed into the ground – any indication of her presence.

The worry was a hard knot inside my belly when I'd covered the ground a second time. She wasn't on the island. And if she wasn't, where in hell could she be? The thought of a boat came into my mind and, mentally rejecting the suggestion, I nevertheless looked out to sea.

Yeah, I should have known there wasn't anything she wouldn't try. And it was only luck that I saw her. She was so far out that from the beach I probably couldn't have seen her head above the swell. Her searching had yielded a discovery: a length of timber, to which she was clinging. I didn't stop to figure how crazy she musta been to begin an eighty-mile swim with only the aid of a plank. Already she musta exhausted herself. She wasn't swimming anymore that I could see, just clinging to the plank.

I raced down to the beach, keeping my eyes on her as long as possible, and ran into the sea, striking out wildly in her direction. She was even farther out than it looked from the island top. I swam so far I began to get scared she'd already gone under, leaving the plank floating on the water, which I wouldn't see until I was on top of it.

Making myself buoyant and gauging the approach of a larger wave, I raised myself out of the water, caught a glimpse of her over to my right.

She couldn't have held on much longer. When I reached her, her arms and chin were resting on the plank and her head drooped wearily so that only with an effort did she manage to raise it when the gentle swell lifted, swamped over her.

I wasn't feeling so happy myself. I'd swum a long way at a killing pace. Now I had to swim back. What was more, I had to get her back too.

Without the plank I couldn't have done it. She was limp, barely conscious, clinging to the plank with only the instinct of survival to give her strength. I turned her on her back, worked the plank under her shoulders. The plank helped give her buoyancy. I took her by the head to support her, swam on my back using my legs for propulsion.

My lungs felt they were bursting, my heart was pounding, and all at once my limbs seemed heavy, as heavy as lead. I kept swimming, kept telling myself it wasn't so far, that pretty soon I'd feel the beach shelving beneath my feet. But my legs grew heavier and heavier, lost all buoyancy, and the swell washing over me got in my mouth, caused me to choke and splutter when my heaving lungs sucked in water instead of air.

I closed my eyes, gritted my teeth, kept my legs moving, moving, moving. I seemed to go on swimming forever. Then, using valuable strength to turn on my side, I discovered that the beach seemed no nearer.

My movements became unconscious agony, an effort that was not part of me. I swam mechanically for an eternity, sustained by a willpower I hadn't the strength to believe in. Then finally my foot touched bottom.

The last few feet required the most desperate effort of all. I hadn't the strength to draw her up the beach. I let her lie half in the water and half out. I lay beside her, exhausted, knowing that never again would I be able to breathe properly, that my tortured lungs could never again suck in enough air to give me life.

I lay there while the water washed around me, listened to the pounding of my heart, slowly, very slowly, easing to a rhythmic pulse. Miraculously my breathing eased, became normal, and the tearing pain in my lungs was soothed. I climbed to my feet, found my legs unsteady and uncertain. Moira was lying there, limp and helpless. It wasn't surprising. She'd been in the water a lot longer than me. She was lucky to touch dry land again.

Life with Moira was plenty exciting. It was plenty exhausting too. Once again I was gonna have to carry her to camp. I did it differently this time, humped her over my shoulder like a sack of coal. It wasn't so good for her dignity and it wasn't so comfortable as being carried in my arms. It wasn't so interesting for me either. But it was a whole lot easier, and the way I felt then, lighting a cigarette was gonna be a real effort.

I got her back to camp, sank down on my knees, let her roll off my shoulder onto the soft sand. That walk had got my heart pounding and my lungs rasping again. It was another fifteen minutes before I summoned the energy to find the Scotch bottle, pour myself a generous allowance.

That day looked like being a repeat of the one before. Moira was unconscious. I spread a blanket for her, made up a pillow and rolled her onto it. I forced whisky between her lips until she moaned. She mumbled something.

'What say?' I growled, putting my ear close to her lips.

'So painful,' she moaned faintly. 'So painful.'

Semiconsciously she moved her hand, and I saw what was worrying her. She lived on the Florida coast, and nobody who lives on the Florida coast in that perfect weather can avoid getting sun-browned. Moira was sun-browned. But local authorities usually have a strong objection to immorality. As a result, there is usually some part of a dame's anatomy that is not sun-browned, instead is a soft, milky white.

Moira's skin was milky white in places usually covered by swim-shorts and sun-top. Her trouble was, she'd over-exposed to the hot sun that sensitive skin rarely exposed. Those parts of her body were now a bright lobster-red, musta been burning like fire after long immersion in salt sea water.

Something had to be done about it. I fed her more whisky, felt her forehead, discovered she was cold. I made up her bed, carried her into the tent. She moaned faintly, complained continually of the pain. I covered her up, and the pressure of the rough blankets against her burned flesh was torment. In a kinda delirium she thrust the blankets away, moaned piteously.

Something had to be done about it!

I forced more whisky between her lips. She was limp, exhausted, able only to move her head faintly from side to side and moan about the pain.

Something had to be done!

I opened up a tin of butter, went back to her, forced more whisky between her teeth. It didn't help any. She was still exhausted, still limp, still semiconscious and still moaning with the pain.

I sighed deeply. I'd undertaken some jobs in my time. But Moira was pulling a few new ones out of the bag for me. I scooped butter from the tin with my hand, waited until it was soft and melting and applied it gently. Her body quivered at my soothing touch. It cooled the burning, took the sting from the salt, gave suppleness to sun-dried skin. After the first few dabs I found it easier. With the tips of my fingers I gently massaged the butter into her skin. Then I used my hand, felt her skin softening and cooling, slipping through my fingers, protected now from the air by a fine film of grease.

When I was through she was still limp, still semiconscious. I pulled the blankets up over her, tucked them underneath her. This time she didn't kick them off. I sat watching her for a long while. She lay quiet, face white, eye-sockets like black caverns. There was nothing more I could do for her except wait until she awoke, wanted something to eat.

The sun was beginning to set. I built up the campfire, started the routine of preparing myself a meal. Afterwards I got out a book, tried to read.

It was like the previous night. I couldn't concentrate on

reading. I kept seeing mental pictures of Moira. They were more unsettling than any I'd had before, linked with the memory of glistening flesh that was slippery to the fingers.

I went to bed knowing it was useless. I'd never get to sleep.

13

It was the third day on the island, the fourth day she'd been without supplies. Once again the smell of frying bacon awakened her. It was incredible how quickly she recovered her strength. The night before, she'd been exhausted. Now she crawled from the tent with a kinda animal litheness. But her face showed clearly the strain she was enduring. Her eyes were dark caverns, nerves in both cheeks twitching, her mouth drooling and open. There was intelligent madness in her eyes as she crawled to the other side of the campfire, waited to be served with food. The calculation in those black eyes was almost frightening, cunning intellect penetrating a screen of madness. I tried not to look at her as she wolfed food, chewed noisily and dirtily. I noticed that my treatment had soothed the sunburn. Her skin was no longer bright red but a softer tone blending into the tan of the rest of her body. It looked like I'd acted in time, that her skin wouldn't peel.

She said, artfully, 'You're strong. You could get me away from here if you wanted.'

I eyed her steadily. 'But I don't want.'

Her face twitched so badly she couldn't speak. She raised her hands to hold it still, and her grease-stained fingers were trembling. It took all of five minutes for the spasm to wear off. Then she said desperately, 'Can't you see? It's killing me. I've gotta have it or I'll die. You've gotta help me.'

'I am helping you,' I said deliberately.

Again her eyes were calculating. 'I'll give you money,' she panted. 'As much as you want. All you've got to do is get me back to the coast. You can be rich. You can live in luxury for the rest of your life.'

I took a long time before replying. 'I like it here,' I said eventually. 'It suits me.'

There was the anger of a child in her when she sprang across the fire at me, beat my chest with her fist and cried with frustration.

I held her off until misery got the upper hand of her rage. She threw herself on the ground, sobbed like her heart would break, her shoulders heaving and big tears rolling down her twitching cheeks. I stood watching her hopelessly. I'd have done anything for her. But there was nothing I could do.

A little later, still sobbing, she scrambled to her feet, stumbled off along the beach, walking as though she was half-blind.

I'd been taught a lesson the previous day. This time I kept an eye on her, followed at a discreet distance, never let her out of my sight.

She wandered aimlessly, as though impelled by some inner force that would not allow her to rest. Three or four times she threw herself on the sand, sat hunched there, sobbing so that even from a distance I could see the heaving of her shoulders. It took a long while, but we made a complete circuit of the island.

When we got back to camp she went into her tent, dropped down on the blankets and sobbed some more.

I cleaned up the breakfast things, prepared lunch. She was ready for food. She was entitled to be. She'd used plenty of energy. It had to be replaced someway.

All through the meal she sat watching me calculatingly with those half-crazed eyes. As soon as she was finished, she went off again. But she didn't go far. She'd started searching again, rooting in the bushes and dried scrub.

I was able to keep an eye on her while I cleaned up the camp. Then I stretched myself luxuriously in the shade of the palm tree, cuddled a bottle of beer and thought how wonderful it would be if only Moira was not ill. I kept my eye on her, could see her moving around. From a distance and with her back toward me, I couldn't see her twitching face and deep-set eyes. I kept thinking of her as a dame. It was unsettling to think of her that way, but I just couldn't stop myself.

It was maybe a coupla hours before she stopped rooting, made a beeline straight for me. I stared as she got closer, sat up straight and gulped. There was purpose in her manner. She came right up to me, knelt down so close I could reach out and touch her if I wanted.

Even wearing only bathing shorts, it was hot in the shade of that palm tree. But a few minutes earlier I'd been ice-cold compared with the way I was sweating now.

She'd been rooting with a purpose. She'd picked long blades of sun-dried grass, plaited them to fashion a small mat. On the mat she'd tastefully arranged soft green moss and tiny colourful flowers. It had been hard work collecting all those little flowers; they grew few and far between. But she'd undertaken that labour to fulfil a purpose. That dainty bed of moss and flowers was a decorative background for her offering. She held the bed on her outstretched palms, held it beneath her breasts, supporting them so they lay soft and feminine, cool, fascinating and sweet-smelling against the flowers.

I swallowed, felt the sweat trickling down the back of my neck, lit a cigarette with a shaking hand.

'They're beautiful, aren't they?' she said softly, huskily.

I wouldn't look at her, concentrated on striking a match. 'Take anything you want,' she urged. 'Take me. You can have money, too. You can do just anything you want.' Half-crazed as she was, she still instinctively realised the appeal woman has to man. She wanted to buy her way to dope, buy me with money, throw herself in as makeweight. Yet it was a calculated action, as cold-blooded salesmanship as the jeweller displaying a diamond necklace against a background of black velvet. This was something I could cope with. But her action showed which way her thoughts were running. It made me think with dread of what might well be the next phase in her cure, the phase when moral consciousness was completely submerged and primitive instincts dominated with all the vigour of her young body.

I got up quickly. She got up too, thrust herself against me. 'You've gotta do it,' she urged desperately. 'I'll go crazy if you don't. And you can have anything you want. You can ...'

I turned away from her, ran down the beach and into the sea. The water was cool. I needed something cooling. I swam around leisurely, watching her closely.

She musta known instinctively she wasn't gonna get me that way. Moreover, desire was cold inside her now. She'd made woman's age-old bid to secure victory over man with woman's weapons. But it was an emotionless bid. Her own desires were dulled by the cravings for a different satisfaction. Her head drooped, so that her black hair dropped over her face. The tiny bed of flowers dropped to the sand and was scattered by an uninterested kick. Then once again she was off along the beach, stumbling half-blindly, crying bitterly with her desire for the unobtainable.

I swam parallel to her, felt her misery so keenly myself that the sun seemed to lose its friendly warmth. Then she sank to the ground, lay there sobbing piteously, and I came out of the water, went over to her.

'Come back with me,' I said gently. 'The sun's too strong to stay in it long.'

She allowed me to help her to her feet, stumbled at my side as I held her arm. The twitching spasms were more frequent now, so her face was perpetually contorted. I could feel her arm shuddering, nerves and muscles jumping and twisting spasmodically and uncontrollably.

I got her back to camp, coaxed her to sit quietly, gave her the butter and told her to use it. She smeared it on herself uninterestedly, black-pained eyes staring in front of her. Strangely enough, I sensed she was suffering more now than the day before, when she'd been wholly animal and oblivious to conscious thought. I dissolved a coupla sleeping tablets in a mug of water, got her to drink it.

It took effect with surprising speed. And now I noticed a

change. Previously when she'd slept, the twitching of her nerves had ceased. Now her face continued to twitch even though she was sleeping.

I made up her bed in the tent, carried her inside and covered her with a thin blanket. Time was the only thing to cure her. Her body needed time to throw off every trace of the drug, cast it out of her system for so long that her body would adjust itself to the lack of it.

Time was her friend and her enemy, and if time could be passed in deep sleep, it would help her considerably.

The sun dipped below the horizon, marking the end of another day. I prepared myself an evening meal and Moira went on sleeping peacefully. I'd awakened early and went to bed early. My sleeplessness of the past two nights was taking its toll. I was tired. I was more tired than I realised. I musta gone to sleep as soon as my head touched the pillow.

It was an abrupt awakening. The blanket ripped off me and weight straddling my bare chest. Yet deep down inside me I was expecting this. I was immediately awake, reaching out for her hands.

Her naked body was burning and moist, her knees gripping my sides urgently, straddling me so that I was enveloped as her arms locked around my neck, drawing my face toward her. She was panting with desperate intensity, her body trembling with vibrant, overwhelming emotion.

She was undergoing another phase in the cure, a phase I'd been dreading, when primitive amorous emotions got beyond control. She'd been cold and without desire earlier. But the idea had been in her mind. It had lingered there, grown until it dominated her. What made it worse was the way I'd been feeling the last few days, and the way I instinctively wanted to respond.

I grabbed her wrists, pulled her arms away from my neck. She twisted her hands free, made use of them, pressed against me urgently and searched greedily for my lips with her own, biting as I tried to turn my head away.

If there'd been a thermometer in my mouth the glass would

have broken and mercury spurted way across the tent. I felt my bones turn to jelly, my body straining toward her and the blood roaring in my ears. For a moment I was poised on the brink of a delirious descent into happiness. Then Rawlins' blue eyes jagged my mind. I made a superhuman effort, rolled her off me, pushed myself into a sitting position.

She came back like a boomerang, but much more so. This time her limbs were strong and winding, her hot hands compelling, her skin burning and slippery.

It was as though my mind was clogged with thick desire, one tiny corner screeching to me what I had planned to do. I knew I'd have to do it quickly, do it right away, otherwise I'd never do it at all.

I got the palms of my hands against her shoulders, thrust hard so that she rolled off me. She was back again at once, hands greedy and clasping. But I'd turned on my belly, was fumbling at the head of the tent beneath my belongings, fingers searching desperately, my mind grimly holding onto the thought that this must be done.

She was panting loudly like a dog as her nails dug into my shoulders, striving to turn me on my back. But I'd found it now, was ready to go with her pulling, rolling so vigorously that she gasped as my weight forced the breath out of her.

She had just one idea in mind. I had a different idea. At first she thought I was in agreement with her, co-operated. Then she realised something was wrong, struggled to get free while I sweated, concentrated on the thing I was doing, finally got the copper girdle around her waist, forced the ends together so that they closed with a loud click.

I sat up, panting desperately. She was a dim shape in the darkness, searching, investigating. 'What is it?' she choked. 'What have you done?'

I breathed hard, said nothing.

She searched some more, suddenly understood. She screamed pantingly, 'Take it off. Get this thing off me.' At the same time, she threw herself about the tent, tearing at the girdle, crazy to get free from it.

John had once again proved his craftmanship. I got up slowly. My mind was still clogged with desire, and that tiny corner of cold reason that was still holding out was screaming to me to take one last action. I still had the key. I crawled out of the tent, ran down the beach and into the water. I closed my eyes, threw the key savagely away from me. It hit the water soundlessly, slipped into the depths. In no time the underwater currents would cover it with sand so that it would lie undisturbed until the end of time.

I went back to the tent and she was crouched there, sobbing with wild frustration. 'Take it off,' she pleaded. 'Take it off.'

'I can't,' I said grimly. 'I haven't got a key …'

'But I can't … we can't …' She broke into a wild paroxysm of sobbing.

I lay there, let her cry it out. But crying wasn't what she wanted. She snuggled closely, clutched me tightly, allowed the wild desire burning inside her to flood through into me.

I held her, comforted her, felt that tiny resisting corner of my desire-swamped mind crushed into nothingness, so that the need inside me was as strong and uncontrollable as hers. It was wonderful to abandon myself completely to my impulses. And it was terrible! It was the frustration of a starving man reaching for a freshly-cooked, steaming and inviting meat pie, knowing invisible glass would deflect his hand before it reached its objective.

Yeah, it was wonderful and it was terrible. It was especially terrible because I myself had foreseen and planned to submit myself to this torment. I was human and I knew my weaknesses. John was a craftsman and I knew his ability. I'd taken a page out of history, absorbed the morality of olden days and ordered the manufacture of a chastity belt[3] that from then on would be my everlasting torment.

---

[3] Author's note: History reveals that chastity belts were in common usage during the Crusades. Fashioned roughly from iron by a blacksmith, painful and uncomfortable to wear, there were nevertheless frequently worn by a Crusader's wife while he was away at the war. Sometimes a Crusader would be away from home as long as three or four years, during which time he was certain of his wife's chastity. She in turn was assured a period of extreme discomfort, chafed by a heavy iron girdle that was her constant companion day and night, while she slept and while she worked. It is not known when this invention of the dark ages fell into disuse. It has, however, been suggested that the statistics on crime climbed swiftly with the introduction of the chastity belt – this because both men and women became adept in the art of picking locks.

14

The next morning she almost killed me.

I'd gone to sleep with her in my arms, strained to me tightly but uselessly. When I awoke I was alone.

I knuckled my eyes sleepily, crawled on hands and knees to the tent door. It was a sixth sense and a warning flicker of shadow on the sand in front of me that saved my life.

Instinctively I rolled to one side, and a huge rock it must have needed all her strength to lift pounded into the sand at my side. She'd been waiting outside the tent for me, had lifted the stone in two hands, poised and brought it smashing down as my head emerged, tortoise-like, from the tent.

That rock could have smashed my skull like an empty eggshell. I rolled three or four times, finished up on my knees facing her. She was quite mad. Her face was contorted, foam at the corners of her mouth. She was staring at the rock, now half-embedded in the sand, with mad exultation shining in her wild eyes. It was as though she could see me lying there, skull smashed, blood and bone spattering the white sand, an awful sight that her mad brain relished.

I got to my feet. 'Take it easy, Moira,' I said, softly. 'Take it easy.'

She looked up at me strangely, wondering how I'd got there, surprise in her eyes. Surprise lasted only a moment. She snarled at me, raised two hands holding an invisible rock, hurled it straight at my head.

'Take it easy, honey,' I soothed. 'Take it easy.'

She snarled again, spun on her heels and ran along the beach. I went after her. She stooped low, ran monkey-fashion toward the palm tree, hands brushing the sand. Maybe it was in her mind to climb that tree. But her senses were out of focus. She ran into it full-tilt, smashed her head against the trunk, fell back on her buttocks, half dazed.

I lifted her to her feet, attempted to soothe her. She slashed my arm in three places with sharp teeth, wrenched herself free and flung herself at the tree. This time she hit it with her shoulder. She bounced back with blood running down her arm from the torn skin, poised to hurl herself once again at the tree.

I got her by the waist, swung her around, sent her spinning so that she lost her balance, sprawled in the sand. She scrambled to her feet, flung herself at me bodily like she thought I was the tree trunk. I slipped to one side, watched her sprawl past me, half-bury herself in the sand. She took longer getting to her feet this time. The first thing she saw was the tree. She flung herself at it. I caught her by the waist, once again sent her spinning to the ground. This time when she climbed to her feet, the breath rasped in her lungs like two pieces of sandpaper being rubbed together. She summoned up the strength to fling herself at me, staggered a coupla paces and collapsed.

She was exhausted and she was crazy. If she didn't kill me, she'd kill herself. There was only one way I knew to prevent either of those things. While she was still weak, her chest heaving as strained lungs sucked in air, I collected ropes from the launch, buried pieces of wood deep in the sand, attached the ropes to them and staked her out. I tied her lying on her back with arms and legs outspread, the ropes slack enough to permit her to move but not so loose that her hands could reach her face or body, tear and lacerate her flesh.

I staked her out where she was, in the shade of the palm tree. When she got stronger and the madness came back on her she strained desperately to get free. The ropes would have cut into her wrists and ankles if I hadn't foreseen what would happen, swathed her flesh with my torn shirt before I tied the ropes.

That was the beginning of the greatest trial I've ever undergone. From then onwards I had to watch her constantly, day and night. When the ceaseless tugging at the ropes failed to satisfy her crazed mind, she twisted her head around, tried to bite pieces from her shoulder. When I held her head, still she chewed her lips so that blood spurted onto the white sand. I wrapped a piece of wood in canvas, forced it between her teeth, pried her jaws apart and bound it securely in position with rope I passed around the back of her neck. Unable now to injure herself, for hour after hour she continued her ceaseless straining at the ropes. The sun rose higher and it got hot. The sweat glistened on her body like she'd been dipped in oil. But her straining, writhing body was never still. It was dark before she lay quietly enough for me to remove the gag, force food between her teeth. Her eyes were wild and staring. She was experiencing no recognisable human emotions. But when food was put in her mouth, she instinctively chewed, became ravenous, held her mouth open for more and more. When she was through eating, she spat out what I gave her, opened her mouth wide and made a spine-chilling mewing noise. I dissolved sleeping tablets in water, poured it carefully into her mouth. It was water she'd been wanting. She gulped it feverishly.

I couldn't run the risk of releasing her. I dragged blankets from the tent, wrapped them under and around her. Because she was drifting off to sleep, I omitted to use the gag. But I had to sit beside her, watching her all the time, ready to gag her again if it became necessary.

It was during the night when the hallucinations started. I was dozing, and she awakened me with a shrill yell of inhuman horror. She was straining to sit up, eyes staring in front of her, dominated by an overwhelming fear. She quivered, thrashed around madly, trying to get free and escape from whatever horror threatened her.

It went on for three days and nights. There were intervals when she was passive enough to eat and drink. Intervals when the sleeping draughts I gave her took effect. There were other times when I gritted my teeth, felt the sweat rolling down my forehead as she thrashed and screamed in piteous terror, living in a strange, horrible dream world of her own, seeing horrible, slimy, crawling things that drove her mind to the limit of breaking point.

I was beside her all the time, never daring to leave her even to get water, except when she was sleeping. The terrible hallucinations and nightmares she experienced were so real to her that they became almost real to me. I half-lived in that nightmare world with her, wanted myself to run madly from the awful apparitions that she alone could see. Her fear was so real that I sensed it. The hairs at the back of my neck would bristle with uncontrollable terror. I lost my appetite, drank too much and found my nerves were shot, so that my fingers twitched and lighting a cigarette was an ordeal.

And then, the fourth morning of the delusions, she was over it. I knew it instinctively, felt it inside me with the same certainty as if I had been inside her body, living with her. We'd been so close together those last few days, we two were almost one.

She was sleeping quietly, white, shrunken and exhausted. I prepared breakfast, dared to wake her. She opened her eyes, blinked in the strong morning light, puckered her forehead and automatically tried to prop herself up on one elbow. The tethering rope around her wrist stopped the movement. She stared blankly, turned to discover what tethered her.

'How are you feeling?' I asked.

Her eyes were startled. 'I'm tied. Why have you done this?'

I didn't answer. I bent over her, released her wrists. She sat up, and the blanket that covered her fell low. She knew at once she was naked, snatched at the blanket, draped it in front of her with a blush suffusing her cheeks. I pretended not to notice, released the ropes around her ankles.

She kept staring at me. There was sullen enquiry in her eyes. I handed her an enamel plate together with a fork. I'd cut up the food so that she could eat it easily. She gathered the blanket around her, ate daintily but hungrily. After a time she said sullenly, 'I've been ill, haven't I?'

'You're almost better now,'

'I've killed it … the craving, I mean.'

'I hope so.'

'I have,' she asserted. 'I haven't got it anymore.' She added quietly, 'I feel so weak, exhausted. I've been through hell.'

'It was worth it.'

'Maybe,' she said. 'Maybe.' She lay back as though exhausted, closed her eyes. She was quiet for so long that I thought she'd gone to sleep again. Then she asked: 'You were with me all the time?'

'I was around.'

'I suppose I ought to thank you,' she said doubtfully.

'You can if you want.'

There was another long silence. 'I guess you had your reasons,' she said bitterly.

I didn't know what she was getting at. I said nothing.

'You stripped me and tied me down,' she said tonelessly. At first I didn't realise what she was thinking. Then I understood. She figured I hadn't tied her for her own good, but for my own amusement.

After what I'd been through, my nerves were ragged. I got mad. 'So you think it was a joyride for me,' I snarled. 'You think I got a kick out of it, huh? You think I enjoyed having you try to kill me, having to save you when you nearly drowned yourself, having to sit by you hour after hour while you suffered delusions, tried to tear yourself to pieces with your teeth.'

Her eyes were wide, startled, staring at me with amazement. 'Is that what happened?'

'You stripped yourself too,' I went on bitterly. 'D'you think that was fun, having you whisk your shape around in front of me day and night?'

She thought that over. Her voice was toneless again. 'You couldn't help yourself, I suppose,' she said bitterly. Her voice broke. 'You had to tie me down?'

I knew it was still in her mind. I was so mad I didn't bother to correct her. 'Aw, quit squawking!' I growled.

She kinda shrunk into herself, lay there watching me with wide, reproachful eyes. I cleared away the breakfast things, went to get water, and she was still lying there when I got back.

'I want to get dressed,' she said.

'You tore your clothes to pieces,' I told her brutally.

'I must wear something,' she protested. 'I can't go around … naked!'

'You have done,' I sneered. 'Why worry now?'

There were tears in her black eyes. 'Haven't you anything I can wear?'

I grunted, went into my tent. I had two shirts. One I wore and a spare I'd brought with me. I gave both to her. 'See what you can do with these,' I growled.

She looked at me expectantly, and I glanced away. I heard her moving around and then a muttered gasp. 'What the hell's this?' she demanded.

She'd put on my shirt, rolled up the sleeves. She hastily pulled the blanket over the lower part of her when I turned around. 'What's eating you?'

'You know … This!'

'What's it look like?'

She kept the blanket around the lower part of her, investigated with her hand, pulled the blanket up as a protective screen around her shoulders so she could investigate with her eyes. When she came up from beneath the blanket, there was a deep red flush to her white cheeks. 'You did this?' she asked, and her cheeks flamed even more brightly.

'You don't have to be embarrassed about it,' I said gruffly. 'You've been ill. In the last few days I've probably seen more of you than you've seen of yourself.'

'How long …? I mean, when did you …?'

'When you got so amorous I couldn't hold you at bay,' I said bluntly.

Her eyes dropped. She said quietly, 'Then it wasn't possible …? You haven't …?'

'Don't thank me,' I snarled. 'I'm human. Thank the girdle.'

She couldn't look at me now. 'I didn't know,' she faltered. 'I didn't think … It was natural that I should have thought …'

'Skip it,' I said wearily. 'Skip it.'

There was a long pause. She asked: 'How do I take it off?'

'There was a key,' I said. 'I threw it in the sea. There's another key in Beach View. You'll have to wait until we get there.'

Her black eyes were wide and indignant. 'You mean I can't get this thing off? You mean I've gotta wear it all the time? You're telling me you were crazy enough to throw away the key …?'

I stared at her levelly. 'You're a nice kid,' I said. 'Even when you're full of dope. And you got mighty persuasive. D'you think it would have been any good fitting that girdle if I'd known where the key was?'

Her eyes dropped shyly. 'I've caused you a lotta trouble, haven't I?'

'You sure have!'

We were out of water again. I carried the stone jar to the top of the mound, filled it, and when I got back, she'd torn off the arms of my second shirt, draped the body of it around her loins like an inadequate sarong. It showed a lot of her left leg and exposed her right thigh almost to the hip. She watched me self-consciously. 'Is it all right?' she asked doubtfully.

'It'll have to be,' I told her. 'There's nothing else.'

She was physically weak after her gruelling experience. For the first two days after her recovery she took things easily, ate a great deal and rested. It was surprising how she blossomed out. For a dainty and feminine dame, she had an amazing constitution. She was intelligent too. While she rested, she got me talking. She was especially interested in what had happened on the island since we'd arrived. Some of the happenings she remembered in a hazy kinda fashion. Other incidents were a complete blank in her mind. But we didn't talk only about her illness. We talked about everything under the sun. There grew between us a bond of understanding. Two more days passed and she was well and healthy, her eyes bright and animated, her movements vigorous and strong, her body lithe and tanned by the sun. She'd gone to work on my shirts, fashioned a sun-top and improved on the waist garment. It didn't cover any more of her, but it was more attractive.

We were living in a paradise. There were two of us alone in the midst of nature, content with each other and finding everything perfect except for one thing.

We sat side by side on the cool sand, our campfire burning brightly and the stars glittering against the black velvet of the night sky. 'You know something, Hank?' she asked, and her bare shoulder moved, touched mine.

'I know a lot of things,' I said. 'They all seem unimportant compared with being here.'

'Me too,' she said. 'I don't want to leave. I want to stop forever.'

'Your father will arrive any day now. Perhaps tomorrow.'

She sighed. 'I suppose there's no chance we could stay …'

I shook my head slowly. 'You can't escape from the world,' I said. 'You wouldn't want to. Right now it would be wonderful … for six months. Not longer.'

She said softly, meaningfully, 'It could be wonderful right now,' and her bare shoulder against mine was electric, her lips ripe and inviting.

I held myself back. I was thinking of Rawlins. 'You're a sweet kid,' I said huskily.

'Why don't you, Hank?' she asked directly. 'Why don't you kiss me? You want to.'

'You know why,' I said shortly.

Her black eyes stared at me penetratingly. 'It was different then,' she said. 'Father knew I was ill. I was at anybody's mercy. But now I know what I'm doing.'

I said, 'Moira,' very softly.

She leaned toward me, and suddenly there was no restraint, her body was hot and throbbing against mine. I was straining her toward me, kissing her eyes, her lips, running my mouth down to her shoulders and neck so that she arched her body and whimpered with pleasure. A little later she said violently, 'Oh, hell!'

I was sweating. 'That's why it was crazy to start,' I said hoarsely.

Her nails were digging into my shoulders. 'We've gotta do something about it,' she panted. 'We've got to. You understand, Hank. I'll go mad otherwise.'

'It's driven me half-crazy already,' I told her.

Her hands were soothing and gentle. 'We'll think of something, Hank,' she promised. 'We'll think of something.'

* * *

'You're sure this is the place?' she asked.

'I'm not sure,' I growled. 'I'm just guessing.'

She sighed. 'Well, we'll work slowly. Mark on the beach each section we cover.'

We'd just finished breakfast and it was unwise to swim on a full stomach, but we were both anxious. We worked toward each other, diving, swimming along the seabed, searching with eyes and fingers for the piece of twisted copper I'd hurled blindly away from me. It was hopeless even before we started. But we had to try. That was the way it was between us. No matter how hopeless, we just had to try.

We were still trying a coupla hours later when I caught sight of the yacht bearing toward the island. 'It's your father,' I told her.

'Hell,' she said. She scowled across the soft swell toward the yacht. We were waist-deep in the sea. Even if we found the key it was too late now.

'He's gonna be pleased to see you fit and well again,' I told her.

'We haven't got much time,' she said quickly. 'What are we going to do?'

'Do about what?'

'About us.'

I stared at her. She stared back. 'You figure this means something?' I asked.

'Don't you?'

'I'm not sure,' I said tiredly. 'I'm not sure.'

'What do you mean, Hank?' she demanded, eyes wide and hurt.

'The way it is,' I said. 'You and me here together, alone. It makes things seem different. But back home you've got friends, rich friends. You can have anything you want, mix with all kinds of people.' I shook my head doubtfully. 'I'm not sure my world is your world. I'm not sure we want the same things, live the same way.'

She leaned toward me, lips parted, white teeth gleaming. 'There's one thing I want, Hank,' she said, seriously, panting slightly. 'I've got no doubt about it. There's one thing I want.'

I nodded toward the rapidly approaching yacht. 'It's a little late,' I said.

'There'll be opportunity,' she said. 'We can fix it.'

The yacht moored a quarter of a mile off the coast. A small motor launch was lowered and came in toward the beach. Rawlins was alone, blue eyes attempting to reduce the distance between us, hand waving a greeting.

We waded chest-deep to meet him, ran the launch up onto the beach, laughing gaily and apparently happy to see him.

He switched off the engine, jumped overboard into water that was waist-deep in his eagerness, waded ashore with total disregard for his expensive clothes. He took Moira's hands, stood staring at her with a wonderful happiness in his eyes. Then he folded her to him, held her tightly. He was laughing and half-crying at the same time. 'You're better,' he choked happily. 'You're really better!'

'She's getting along fine,' I told him. 'Maybe she wants feeding up a little. But she's doing fine.'

He held her closely, affectionately. 'You've made a fine job, son,' he said. 'I'm real grateful to you. And if there's …' He broke off, his brow puckered. His fingers around Moira's waist moved, probed. 'What the hell …?' he began.

Moira said quickly, 'It's a girdle. Hank will explain.'

He stared at her, he stared at me. His blue eyes were wondering.

I took him by the arm, led him up the beach. 'You see, it's this way,' I began. 'You didn't want anyone to take advantage of Moira. Neither did I. But I'm just as human as the next guy, and …'

15

Rawlins' yacht got us back to the coast by evening. He'd already warned me that there were telegrams awaiting me that he'd taken the liberty of bringing up from my villa. Moira's first preoccupation was to go to her room, get into some clothes. My first interest was those telegrams.

They were from the Chief, about a dozen of them. He'd been sending them at two-hourly intervals. The message in each was more or less the same: 'Return immediately to Chicago.'

I checked up on the air timetables, found I could catch a plane at 7.00 the next morning. Then I put through a trunk call to Chicago.

'What the hell's been keeping you?' growled the Chief. 'I've been going crazy trying to contact you.'

'You're contacting me now,' I said. 'What the hell do you want?'

'Something big's cropped up,' he said. 'It's really big. I want you to handle it.'

'Look, Chief,' I said ominously. 'I'm on holiday. Remember? It was your idea.' While I was speaking I was thinking of Moira, remembering her black eyes, the promise in her smile and the way my temperature had been bounced up and down that last two or three weeks without any satisfactory development.

'Don't argue with me, Janson,' he thundered. 'This is urgent. Nobody else can handle this except you. You catch the first plane back.'

I scowled. 'It's in the morning,' I said.

'Catch it,' he ordered. 'Even if you have to crucify yourself, catch that plane in the morning!'

There's no arguing when the Chief is in a mood like that. I hung up, glared moodily at Rawlins.

'Trouble?'

'Gotta leave in the morning,' I grunted. 'Something special. Won't tell me what it is.'

He took a deep breath. 'Janson,' he said, 'I want you to know how grateful I am for everything you've done. If it hadn't been for you ...'

He went on talking. I wasn't listening. I was thinking of Moira. This was her first night back and it was my last night there. I knew what I wanted. Moira knew what she wanted. It was the same thing. But it wouldn't be that night. And to hang around watching Moira would aggravate my temperature beyond endurance. There was only one thing to do: beat it before Moira finished changing.

'Look,' I said quickly. 'I've gotta go. I've gotta be packed and ready to leave early in the morning.'

'But you can't,' he protested. 'You've only just got back, and ...'

I eyed him steadily. 'I've gotta go,' I said. 'I'm sorry to appear rude I've gotta go.'

'But, Hank,' he protested. 'You've gotta let me do something. You've helped me, and if there's anything ...'

'I've told you what I want,' I said. 'Your daughter's better. There's a guy that fixed it so nothing happened you didn't want. You do what you can for him.'

'Sure,' he said. 'Sure I'll fix that, Hank. But I want to do something for you too. Now, if you'll ...'

I brushed him off. I was brusque, almost rude, accepted gruffly his offer to be driven back to my villa by his chauffeur.

It was quiet in my villa, lonely. I couldn't stop thinking of Moira. I helped myself to a strong whisky, got out my suitcases and slowly packed. I was pouring myself another drink when the telephone rang. I swore softly to myself. It was probably the

Chief. I picked up the receiver, bawled into it, 'What the hell do you want now?'

'You, Hank,' she said softly.

I didn't speak for a long while. I stood there, trying to stop my heart pounding. Finally I said hoarsely, 'It's no good, Moira. I've gotta leave tomorrow. I couldn't stand seeing you again.'

'You're forgetting something.'

'I'm not forgetting anything.'

'Yes, you are,' she said. 'I'm still locked in this damned thing. I want the key.'

This was something that had to be taken care of. 'I'll get it for you,' I said. 'I'll send it along.'

'Don't bother,' she said coldly. 'Just get it. I'll send somebody for it later.'

'In a coupla hours.'

'That'll do.'

She hung up and I stood there holding the dead receiver in my hand, feeling I was dead myself. But it was the way it had to be. I found my fedora, crushed it on my head and made for John's place.

Jane was there too, just getting ready to go off to the show. They both looked at me approvingly. 'You had a nice trip,' said Jane.

'Fine,' I said.

'You look well,' said John. 'Really sunburnt.'

'That's fine,' I said dully.

'What's biting you?' asked Jane.

'Got a lot on my mind,' I said. 'I've little time to spare. I'm packing now, got to leave for Chicago tomorrow.'

Jane's face fell. 'What a pity,' she said sincerely.

John said, 'Yeah, what a pity. We'd have liked to have seen more of you.'

I held my hand toward him. 'You know what I want.'

'Yeah, sure.'

He dug down in a drawer, handed me the key. One eyebrow was slightly raised. 'I've figured out what that thing was,' he said.

I shot a swift glance at Jane. She wasn't listening. He intercepted my glance, understood it. 'I've figured it out for myself,' he said meaningfully. I knew then he hadn't told Jane about it.

I flushed. 'It was an idea I had.'

He looked me up and down, the corner of his mouth twitched. His grey eyes laughed. 'You've got me puzzled,' he admitted.

'Stay that way,' I told him. 'It's served its purpose, worked better than I ever believed possible.'

'You must tell me about it sometime.'

'Maybe I will,' I said. 'Maybe!'

I shook hands with him, said goodbye to Jane. She came to the door with me and I closed one eye at her, jerked my head imperceptibly to show I wanted to talk to her. She caught on quickly, said in a casual voice, 'I'll come down and show you out.'

'Don't bother,' I said. 'I'll find my way.'

'No bother,' she insisted. 'Won't be a moment, John.'

At the foot of the stairs I took her arm fiercely. 'Don't ask questions, Jane,' I said. 'But pretty soon a medical faculty is going to get in touch with John, offer to examine him and perform the operation free of charge, as long as there's a chance.'

She tensed all over. 'What are you talking about?' she said coldly.

My fingers gouged into her arm. 'Don't ask questions,' I growled. 'That's just the way things are gonna work. If he wants that operation, he can have it. It won't cost him anything.'

There was another long pause. 'Hank,' she said, in a faint voice. 'I'm scared. It's a dangerous operation. I keep worrying in case …'

'Who are you to stand in his way?' I rasped. 'Who are you to worry? It's his life. He knows what he wants. You mustn't stand in his way.'

'D'you think I'd do that?' she asked quietly.

'Yeah,' I said bluntly. 'You'd rather he didn't take the

chance. You'd talk him out of it if you could. And maybe you could, at that.'

'For his sake,' she moaned softly. 'For his sake.'

I was brutal with her. 'Who are you to decide?' I demanded. 'You love him. Sure you love him. You love him too much. He's been taking risks all his life. Yet you wouldn't let him take just one more. Not even if to him it meant living again.' I worked a bitter note into my voice. 'It's not him you love so much, it's yourself.'

She was numbed, hurt by my words. She drew in her breath sharply, tried to suppress a sob. 'You think he should …?'

'Listen, Jane,' I said sincerely. 'He mustn't know this. But there's a guy interested in him, a guy with dough. John will get the best medical advice, the best surgeons. Everything that's possible will be done. It's an opportunity he can't afford to miss. You mustn't let him miss it, either.'

It was gloomy in the passage. But I could see the shine in her moist eyes. 'You think it'll be all right, Hank?'

I fanned her chin with my fist playfully. 'Sure, it'll be all right, kid. Just let him decide what he wants.'

'I don't know what to say,' she stammered. 'I don't know how I can thank …'

'Forget it,' I said.

She came close. 'I'll always remember you, Hank.'

'I'll always remember you,' I said.

There was a long pause. We stared at each other through the gloom of the passageway. I was remembering her on that platform, clinging satin blouse against jutting breasts. I could sense now the suppressed throbbing inside her. 'Well, goodbye, Jane,' I said.

'Goodbye, Hank.'

We still stood there; we were both burning, both wanting yet not wanting to do something about it.

She turned abruptly, fled up the stairs without a backward glance, as though she was scared of herself. I could sympathise. I was scared of myself too.

I let myself out, strode back to my villa, walking as fast as I could to help let off steam.

It was lonely when I got back there; much more lonely than I ever remembered it being. So lonely I was wishing it was morning and I could be catching my plane. I poured myself a Scotch, heard the veranda step creak. I froze, glass in mid-air, and watched the French windows.

They opened slowly, and she stood there framed in the doorway, staring at me with black, expressive eyes.

'Hello, Hank,' she said.

She was worth staring at. She'd changed into an evening gown, one of those she'd been telling me about. The bodice fitted like a tight sheath, only half ensnaring her breasts, pulled up beneath them tightly to make them swell and thrust. The black skirt was full, flared outwards from her neat waist.

I gulped. 'Hiya, Moira.'

'Can I come in?'

She was as good as in already. I nodded dumbly. She smiled softly as she closed the doors behind her. The movement of her arms and shoulders caused her breasts to move, rippling her soft flesh with liquid motion.

'Nothing to say, Hank?' she asked softly.

'Yeah,' I said. 'How about a drink?'

'Scotch,' she said, and the way she was looking at me, I knew she didn't care if she had a drink or not.

I turned, got another glass from the cabinet, poured her a drink. She was watching me all the time.

'Why did you run away, Hank?'

I pushed the drink across the table toward her, and as she glided forward to take it, she was all soft black eyes and swelling breasts.

'It was the best way,' I said gruffly. 'You're back home now. I've got to leave in the morning. That's the way life is. It's better to break it up now than later, because later maybe it'll hurt too much.'

'You're a fool, Hank,' she said softly.

'Just the same, I get along.'

'You're a fool,' she repeated.

I flushed. 'I'll give it to you straight,' I said. 'What way d'you want this to be? We live in different worlds, we live different lives. I had a tough time on the island with you. But nothing happened. Why spoil everything? If I clear out now, nothing will ever happen. Why cheapen it, make it something casual and fly-by-night?'

She moved around the table, came so close that those semi-revealed mounds were prodding my chest. Her eyes were hot and sulky, moist red lips parted to show gleaming teeth. She extended one hand, rested it gently on my hip. I sweated and quivered at her touch.

'You're a fool, Hank,' she said for the third time.

'Cut it out, Moira,' I pleaded. 'Go home, will ya?'

'Why be blind?' she asked. 'You're like me.'

She meant that I wanted her as badly as she wanted me. That was no lie. And I no longer had any wish to fight her off. I slipped my arm around her, felt the strength go out of her body and surge into her mouth. Her lips were ripe, passionate and burning.

'That was wonderful, Hank,' she murmured, relaxing in my arms.

'That was goodbye,' I told her gruffly. 'Now beat it.'

Those black, slumberous eyes were gleaming invitingly through half-closed eyelids. 'When does your plane go, Hank?'

'Seven o'clock in the morning.'

She moved her body against mine, irresistibly and subtly. Somehow the bodice lost ground too. Her frock was thin, I could feel her skin burning through it. There was that familiar hot, sensuous clogging of my mind. It seemed that no matter how much I wanted, I could never get enough of her.

'Your plane leaves at 7.00,' she repeated huskily. 'Did you remember to get the key?'

'Sure, I got it,' I said hoarsely.

'Well, what are you waiting for?' she demanded angrily. 'Why are we wasting time?'

Other Crime Titles available from Telos Publishing

HANK JANSON
Classic pulp crime thrillers from the 1940s and 1950s.
TORMENT
WOMEN HATE TILL DEATH
SOME LOOK BETTER DEAD
SKIRTS BRING ME SORROW
WHEN DAMES GET TOUGH
ACCUSED
KILLER
FRAILS CAN BE SO TOUGH
BROADS DON'T SCARE EASY
KILL HER IF YOU CAN
LILIES FOR MY LOVELY
BLONDE ON THE SPOT
THIS WOMAN IS DEATH
THE LADY HAS A SCAR
BABY, DON'T DARE SQUEAL
MILADY TOOK THE RAP
THE JANE WITH GREEN EYES

For full details of all Telos titles, please visit our website at
www.telos.co.uk where there are facilities for worldwide credit
card online ordering.

www.ingramcontent.com/pod-product-compliance
Lightning Source LLC
Chambersburg PA
CBHW072150170626
46813CB00004BA/1751